# This Book Belongs To:

_____

_____

First published 2021 © Twinkl Ltd of Wards Exchange,
197 Ecclesall Road, Sheffield S11 8HW

ISBN: 978-1-914331-41-1

MIX
Paper from
responsible sources
FSC® C013056

We're passionate about giving our children a sustainable future, which is why
this book is made from Forest Stewardship Council® certified paper.
Learn how our Twinkl Green policy gives the planet a helping hand at
www.twinkl.com/twinkl-green.

Printed in the United Kingdom.

10 9 8 7 6 5 4 3 2 1

A catalogue record for this book is available from the British Library.

A TWINKL ORIGINAL

# Percy Poll's Peculiar Plants

Twinkl Educational Publishing

# Contents

# Chapter One

It had been quite the morning at Poll Manor. Percy had taken his usual seat at the breakfast table, doodled roses idly in his notepad and watched as the chaos had begun to unfold.

As he observed his family, he saw Father burn through his third saucepan, trying to scramble eggs. Basil Poll rattled around the kitchen, too tall for his own good. He knocked utensils over with his too-long arms, bashed into open cupboard doors with his too-knobbly knees and tripped over the dog with his too-big feet.

It appeared that, sometime earlier that morning, Mother had tidied away the butter, which had drastically affected how quickly he had burnt the eggs. When Mother was unable to find the butter again, Father gave up and served bread with prune jam instead.

"Breakfast is the most important meal of the day! It prepares you for whatever is to come. Fail to prepare; prepare to fail – that's what I always say!" he declared as he sprinkled dried parsley over his serving.

Mother eventually found the butter in her knitting bag. Bratwurst reminded her that it was there by sticking his long snout into the collection of coloured twine for a lick.

"The wool protects it from the flies," Mother said, "but not from dachshunds, apparently."

Mother had a gentle way of being. She had a heart-shaped face with large, dark eyes and her thick hair, streaked with grey, was always held off her face by a silk scarf. She seemed to breeze around the house as if her feet floated a few centimetres above the floor. She always wore one of her many huipils – today's was the one with the stitched flowers around the neck and the red trim. Percy thought she looked like a patch of valerians. When Mother looked at Percy, he felt like he was the only person in the world.

Grandmother believed, and often said, that she thought that Mother was odd. This was, no doubt, down to Mother's habit of tidying things away in surprising places and her unusual beliefs about how the house should be kept. Many years ago, for example, Mother had installed a thermometer in every room of the house and still spent much of her time checking each one to make sure that the inside of Poll Manor stayed the perfect temperature for brain function – which, according to her, was twenty-and-a-quarter degrees Celsius. Mother had her ways, but Percy never complained when he found various sugary snacks in his bed.

"So that you will have sweet dreams," she would say happily.

Percy cleared his plate and escaped into his favourite room in the house: the orangery. The orangery was the only part of the house where Percy was rarely disturbed, as it contained nothing but plant life and was of no interest to the rest of the Poll family. Tall, narrow windows stretched from floor to ceiling along the walls of the large room, which stuck out from the rest of Poll Manor to get sunlight on three sides. This light was now limited, however, due to the amount of grime that had collected on the flat, glass roof and the sheer volume of exotic plants that filled every corner of the space. A date palm towered over everything and the luscious lemon and orange trees gave the shady room a wonderful citrus aroma. Percy leant close to the creeping jasmine to block out the smell of Father's cooking.

For a moment, Percy took in his own faded reflection in a dusty, gold-framed mirror that was propped against the wall. His large, goggle-like glasses rested on the tip of his nose. Just like his father, Percy needed them for reading, writing, looking and just about everything else. Also, just like his father, he had never managed to find a pair that fit. His dark, tightly curled hair sat atop his head as usual; it always seemed to grow faster than he could trim it. Today, he wore his summer suit with the bow tie and waistcoat. Mother said that it made him look handsome but Percy was not so sure.

As he looked at himself, he wondered where Daisy was. His sister had not come down for breakfast. He had not heard her usual banging and clattering so far that morning, and –

"Hey! Percy Petal!"

Daisy landed with a thump through the open, glass-panelled doors that led to the grounds, almost as if she had swung in on one of the hanging vines. She shook her head and a cloud of dust and dirt bloomed out in all directions. She wore her usual pair of tatty, denim work dungarees and brought in a smell of grease and engine oil. When she took a second to look at Percy, her brow creased into a frown in the way that it did with all the women of the Poll family.

"Don't call me Petal," Percy said. He watched his sister stride farther into the room. Daisy was, as Grandmother would say, 'a scruffy menace'. Where Grandmother, who lived on the uppermost floor of Poll Manor, demanded dresses, make-up and handbags, Daisy wore old boots, gloves and a toolbelt.

"It's warm in here," she complained, tugging at the neck of her sweater.

"Don't tell Mother," Percy replied. "The plants in here like it warm."

"What's that smell?" asked Daisy, crinkling her nose.

"Breakfast," Percy replied, sniffing the burnt air.

"Oh dear. Another of Dad's creations gone wrong!' she said, rolling her eyes. "Come on, Petal. Let's get out of here."

Together, they ran from Poll Manor and down the many steps into the garden. The wide, sloping lawns stretched down from the main house to the vast green below. Once, the rolling landscape had been neatly mowed. The two of them would have spent hours tumbling down until they grew sick, tired or both.

The estate had been in the Poll family for

generations. The place seemed to have a mind of its own, though, and over the years, it had become a constant battle between the owners and the house. The family had admitted defeat long ago and it had become wild beyond words. The house itself was crumbling like a week-old biscuit and the only person that seemed to care enough to do something about it was Daisy. Percy usually left her to it and instead, turned his attention to the gardens, which were now tall, willowy, entwined messes.

"Where are we going?" Percy asked through heavy, exhausted breaths.

"To see the flowers! I want the guided tour."

Percy wanted to complain about being dragged this way and that, but Daisy was older and taller than him so she was definitely in charge. Besides, he loved any opportunity to talk about the plants of Poll Manor.

"OK," Percy said as he drew level with her. "We'll start with the agapanthus."

\*

Nearly an hour later, at the far reaches of the manor's grounds, Percy and Daisy followed a shrub border towards the lake.

"The professor told me that there's a monster in there," Percy said. Rumour had it that there was a giant sea squid or terrible kraken living in the still waters. Admittedly, the worst Percy had ever seen there was a thick layer of gloopy, green algae but he continued to live in hope.

"The professor told *me* that the moon is thirty-eight per cent Swiss cheese. You can't listen to a word he says," Daisy replied.

They continued to walk along the shrub border. It had once been attached to a low, iron picket fence. Now, it was entangled with wild vines and roses of pink, white and the deepest of reds. Huge clumps of meadowsweet bloomed through the fence. Mother said that it was the most terrible weed.

"What is a weed?" Percy had asked her one morning as she had busied herself with arranging the cutlery in chronological order.

"A weed, my little petal, is a wild thing growing where it has no right to be. Everything must have its place."

Percy smiled ironically to himself as he remembered watching his mother happily moving on to reorder the crockery. He looked at his sister, who held the petal of a flower lightly in her fingers.

"What are these called again?" Daisy asked as she pushed her nose into the blush-pink flower.

"That's a peony." They wandered on a few steps.

"And this one?"

"That's a rose."

"What about this?" Daisy said, squatting down.

Percy frowned. "That's grass."

"And this?" Daisy replied, grabbing a handful of something damp and brown.

"That's soil, with a sprinkling of compost."

Daisy rose to her feet. She towered over him. "Are you sure?"

"Of course I'm sure. I spread it yesterday. Look, you can still see some of Father's fried custard in the mix."

Daisy raised it to her face to get a closer look. "Be careful," Percy warned. "He used a lot of chilli in this batch. In fact, I think he used *all* the chilli."

"I think your glasses are fogged over again. You need a closer look. Here!" Daisy lunged forwards with her hand and aimed the compost straight at Percy's face. At the last moment, he ducked out of her way and under her sweeping arm. There was at least one benefit to being on the small side.

"Come back, Petal!" Daisy called, mischief in her words. "We need to plant you so you'll grow."

Percy took one look over his shoulder as he ran and grinned. "You'll have to catch me!"

He weaved between the border plants, aiming

for the conifers and the lake beyond. Daisy was quick but he was clever. Cutting through the dense vines and brambles, Percy managed to stay just out of her reach. Like a weed, he found his way somewhere he did not belong as he headed deeper into the thicket.

When, at last, Daisy launched another handful of compost through the brambles, Percy knew he had won. As he breathed a sigh of relief, a *whizz*, a *boom* and a *crash* came from the direction of the manor.

"Uh-oh!" Daisy said, looking at her watch. "Dad must be in the kitchen again."

With that, she turned and ran in the direction of Basil Poll's latest cooking catastrophe. Percy watched, knowing that, whatever had happened, Daisy would sort it. She had a special power for being in the right place at the right time. Where everyone else looked for problems, Daisy was the solution.

Percy took a moment to enjoy the mid-morning sunshine and the birdsong filling the air. He rested on the crisp grass and leant back on his hands but, just out of the corner of his eye, something caught his attention. A small shoot was growing out of the ground and he had narrowly avoided crushing it with his hand. It was the most curious, peculiar plant that Percy had ever seen.

Calling on his greatest botany knowledge, Percy observed the small sprout. Not only did it have multiple stems but its leaves were thorny, its berries were dark and clumped together, and it seemed to be *moving*. As Percy leant in for a closer look, he realised that it wasn't the gentle breeze that was causing it to move: the plant appeared to be travelling across the ground, using its roots like tiny legs.

"Wow!" Percy whispered, scooping the plant and a handful of dirt into his shirt pocket. "You're coming with me."

# Chapter Two

The plant had repeatedly attempted escape. Three times, it had leapt free as Percy had walked back to the house. The first time, it had slipped out of his breast pocket, using its leaves as a parachute and landing among the lavender. Percy had waited for the plant to break cover and try to run for freedom before he had caught it.

The second time, it had used its roots to crawl over Percy's shoulder and down his back. Percy had felt the tiny root hairs tickling his neck and had carefully picked it up before it had managed to get any farther.

The third time, having now been put inside the pocket of Percy's shorts, the plant had used its thorny leaves to slice through the lining and slide to freedom. Only when Percy had felt soil trickling down his leg had he stopped, scooped up the plant and closed it inside an empty jam jar that Mother had apparently hidden inside a patch of snapdragons. 'To catch the perfumed air,' Percy supposed.

With the plant now quiet, Percy passed back through the orangery and into the kitchen. The large room was empty and the air smelt clean, which meant that Daisy had got to Father just in time. Percy walked past the wooden-topped counter in the middle and the area that held the antique dining table.

"What do you have there, Percival?" Father suddenly emerged from the scullery at the far end of the kitchen. Apparently, he had been spending some time with his pots and pans.

"Nothing!" Percy lied.

Father walked towards the counter. "Something to add to lunch, perhaps?" He collected the peeler from the drawer and began to toss apples into the air. As they fell, Father slashed at them with the peeler and they bounced one by one across the kitchen. "Gravity-enhanced peeling," he said, noting the look on Percy's face. "It stops them browning. Now, tell me. What do you have in that jar?"

"It's nothing, Father, truly. It is not an ingredient."

"Oh, Percival," Father said as the last apple fell and rolled across the floor. "Everything is an ingredient if you add the right spices. Here, have a sniff of this." Father reached under the kitchen counter and produced a thimble-sized, glass jar. It had a cork stopper and was filled with an earth-coloured powder.

"What is it?" Percy asked warily.

"It's my new spice mix. Give it a sniff. I'm sure you'll pick up the hint of acorn."

Percy raised the pot to his nose and pretended to

16

take a big sniff. Despite leaving the stopper on, he could still feel the mix of spices attacking his throat. "Lovely!" he said. "Smells like squirrel."

Father smiled and then turned to his oven, knocking his head on a series of hanging pans and creating a sound like that of a xylophone.

Percy left the room and rounded the door into the corridor with its wall of family portraits. Then, he climbed the grand staircase and reached the top in several huge leaps and bounds. Outside Daisy's bedroom, he skidded to a halt at the sight of an oblong-shaped creature on short legs. It barrelled towards him from the spiral staircase at the end of the corridor, which led up to the second floor and, beyond that, Grandmother's attic.

"Bratwurst!" Percy called in surprise as the family dachshund hurtled past him and down the stairs leading to the ground floor, leaving a trail of yellow, painted paw prints behind him. The last glimpse Percy got was of a brown overcoat and of a deerstalker hat tied under the sausage dog's chin. Grandmother, the family portrait artist, had obviously begun to add another painting to her latest oil paint project: 'The Life and Times of Bratwurst Poll'.

Percy arrived at his bedroom on the first floor, pushed open the heavy, wooden door and entered. The light hit him instantly. Percy's room had windows from one wall to the other that looked out over the grounds and to the lake beyond. It was in the perfect position to watch the summer sun rising over the horizon.

Percy's bed faced the door with the headboard against the wall of windows. His bed welcomed him whenever he strode into the room. Mother had decided on this layout as she said that he would grow faster with his head towards the sun. Percy liked it for another reason. He took a short run-up and leapt with one arm outstretched, the other holding the jar and his legs spread wide. He landed with a *pop*.

Wait a second... *pop*?

Cautiously, Percy crawled off the bed and put his hand under the sheets. It came out dusty. He sniffed his fingers. They smelt of lemon sherbet.

"Sweet dreams..." he sighed, as he imagined Mother placing the bag of sweet dust into his sheets at some point that morning.

THUD, THUD, THUD. From above, a series of booming sounds filled the room. Grandmother, despite being older than anyone knew, had exceptionally good hearing. With her ear trumpet, she had an almost perfect ability to hear all the noises in the house. She was especially good at hearing Percy's noises.

Next came a muffled cry. "WILL YOU BE QUIET?!"

Percy stood beside his bed with the jar containing the plant cradled to his chest. He raised the glass container so he could get a clear look. Since he had scooped it out of the ground and brought it inside, the plant had begun to droop and wilt.

"Do you need more oxygen?" Percy wondered.

He unscrewed the top of the jar and a whoosh of air seemed to flood in. At that, the plant suddenly perked up and straightened itself upright.

Percy's eyes widened. He knew that oxygen was essential to plants but he had never seen one react so quickly. The plant gave its leaves, berries and stem a good, hard shake, like Bratwurst might after a downpour. Then, with a great leap, it spiralled out of the jar, flew through the air and buried itself into his bedroom wall.

"Wow!" Percy exclaimed. He moved closer to the plant, taking in the sight of it as its tiny, spindly roots disappeared into the plaster. Percy watched as small cracks appeared and began to

spread across the wall. "Uh-oh," he muttered. "I need to find Daisy."

*

"Oh, Petal. What have you done?"

"It wasn't my fault! The thing just jumped into the wall."

Daisy looked down at him, her face smeared in soot. "It jumped?"

"Um, well, yeah," Percy said, trying to remember exactly what had happened.

Daisy took a deep breath and then moved closer to the plant. It seemed to react to her face, almost leaning towards her as she leant towards it.

"Careful!" warned Percy, reaching out to hold her back.

Daisy waved him away and angled her face even closer. Percy craned his head to the side and pushed his glasses up the bridge of his nose. He held his breath and waited.

"Look at those berries," Daisy exclaimed, reaching her hand out to touch them. Percy knew that this could be dangerous and leapt to push her hand away. "OK, OK," she protested, backing off. "Chill out."

"I need to catalogue it and those berries might be poisonous. Some are if you touch them, you know," Percy explained. "Also, if you put your greasy fingers all over it, I won't be able to make accurate observations."

"Fine, fine, fine. Well, in that case, you'll have to sort it out yourself. Just make sure it doesn't get into the plumbing. I've only just got all the sprout pudding out."

With that, Daisy hurried to leave the room. As she did, her foot cracked a floorboard and she nearly went straight through.

"Woodworm," she muttered, pulling her left leg free. Then, without hesitation, she removed a hammer and nails from her belt, reset the board and hammered it back into place.

Percy watched as his sister took a moment to reflect on her work. "Good enough," she said. "Be careful on that one, Petal."

As Daisy disappeared, Percy decided to look a little closer at his discovery. He took in the compound leaves, which seemed to be enjoying the midday sunshine that poured in through the windows. They were similar to those of the umbrella plant that Percy enjoyed so much in the orangery. Yet, unlike the graceful umbrella plant, this plant had thorns on its leaves. There were around half a dozen running down the purple midvein. They looked like a row of fangs waiting to strike.

The berries hung from the top of the two stems just underneath the purple leaves. There were three on each and they were so dark red that they almost glowed. Percy could understand why Daisy had been so drawn to them. Inside each one, Percy knew, were seeds which held the potential, if released, to produce even more plants. In the natural world, it was usually a plant's aim to make its berries as attractive as possible to animals who might help to spread the seeds around the area.

Percy then looked to the wall and touched his hand to the cracks caused by the spreading root system. They splintered off in all directions and the roots seemed to be burrowing deeper and deeper into the plaster.

"Right," Percy said. He squinted at the plant and took a few seconds to observe it swishing and swaying lightly. "This is serious... Where's my botany box?"

# Chapter Three

After lunch, Percy scuttled through the corridors of the great house, opening drawers, looking behind portraits and sticking his head in vases – but he repeatedly came up empty-handed.

"Where *is* it?"

The box containing Percy's botany tools had once belonged to his grandfather. For a few years, Mother had used it to store items rhyming with steel: peel, eel and a pair of stiletto shoes. Now, it was Percy's but it had a nasty habit of getting lost when he needed it most.

Percy blew a strand of straggly hair away from his eyes and tried to remember the last time he had seen the old, steel box. In it, he kept his paper, pencils, clippers and magnifying glass. With the strange plant stuck in his wall, he would need them more than ever.

As he racked his brain, the longcase clock near the foot of the staircase chimed one loud, lengthy chime, which meant that Percy's lessons with Professor Devereux were due to begin.

Professor Devereux was, and had always been, the live-in family tutor. He had held this position longer than anyone knew. Apparently, he had taught Grandmother everything she knew and had been an old man even then.

Professor Devereux's lessons took place in the manor's enormous library on the second floor. As far as Percy knew, the old man only left his private chambers in the west wing to teach Percy and Daisy. He had a long, white beard and was older than the bricks and mortar of Poll Manor. There were many rumours and myths about

Professor Devereux. If you were to believe them all, as Percy did, then Professor Devereux was born in the time of King Arthur, was an expert in swordsmanship, invented the trombone and could read the periodic table in fourteen different languages. Whether or not this was true, what *was* true was that Professor Devereux was strict on timings and school was about to begin.

Percy took the spiral stairs two at a time, ran along the second-floor corridor past his parents' bedroom, turned left and skidded to a halt at the engraved, oaken door of the library. He took a deep breath, moved a step closer to the door and pressed his ear against it.

At first, there was nothing. Then, Percy heard a faint sound. A shuffling? A rolling? Percy leant back on his heel and the board beneath him groaned heavily. From above, three angry thuds echoed through the house.

"WILL YOU BE QUIET?!" a raspy voice whistled through the cracks in the ceiling.

The door to the library blew open and a bony but fierce hand sprang out and landed on

Percy's wrist.

As Percy was dragged into the library, Professor Devereux's parchment face met his and Percy noticed that his beard was flecked with crumbs. Professor Devereux was the only member of the household who enjoyed Father's cooking and, judging by the smell of his breath, he seemed to have polished off the last of Father's lunchtime concoction of pilchard soup and nettle scones.

Professor Devereux used a wheelchair but Percy was not sure if it could still be called that. The professor had added so many new and amazing features that it had become an invention all of its own. It seemed to be powered by steam, due to

E=MC²

28

the vertical pipes that gave off a white cloud every few seconds. The professor also never touched the wheels as the chair moved on its own after the tap of a few buttons.

"Master Percival," he said, each word a croak. "You are late."

"Sorry, Professor."

Professor Devereux scowled at him and clicked his tongue. "Apologies don't unsqueeze the oranges, young master. Take your seat. We must begin our lesson."

"But I haven't got my trombone, Professor."

"Not to worry, Master Percival. Today, we shall have *fun*." The final word sounded strange coming from the professor, as though it tasted peculiar to him.

"Fun?" Percy repeated cautiously.

"Oh, yes. Today, we learn the history of medieval roads." The professor raised his bushy eyebrows, which looked like two hairy caterpillars struggling to get free, and stared intently at Percy, who groaned.

"Didn't we learn about that last time?"

"Oh, no," Professor Devereux smiled. "That was medieval *paths*. These are like paths but wider." Happily, he held his hands about a shoulder's width apart to show Percy what 'wider' meant. This was going to be a long lesson, Percy thought.

Inside the vast library, Percy breathed in the smell of the aged books which lined every wall, carefully placed in rows on antique bookshelves. Daisy said that they smelt like wet dog but, to Percy, they were entire worlds bound in leather and the musty smell held only in old books was the first step into adventure. They were portals into what could be. The only person who loved books more than Percy was Professor Devereux, who could always be counted on to know exactly where to find any volume you needed.

Tall ladders stood attached to the shelves. They were of no use to the professor, whose incredible chair was equipped with the most wonderful motorised arms and hydraulic levers to enable him to reach the right book. Percy, however, used to love sliding on them from left to right and jumping off at the last minute before they crashed into the walls. That game had been stopped by Mother when one of the ladders had carried on going off the shelf, through the window and down onto Father's motorcar. It was still there and made trips into town particularly uncomfortable, especially when it rained.

Atop the bookshelves were some of the Poll family's most prized possessions: ornate vases, busts of historical figures and one bright yellow teapot. ("What's more valuable than a cup of tea?" Mother had said.)

Percy took his place at the angular, wooden writing desk that was framed by the library windows. For many generations, this desk had supported some of the greatest thinkers of the Poll family. Percy knew that his ancestors had sat at the wide, sturdy table and created wonderful works: novels, sonnets, operas. Percy gently moved a loose sheet of paper away from an inkwell, revealing a carving from his grandfather's grandfather, Ernesto Poll – the greatest and most visionary architect of his time.

'ERNIE WOZ ERE – 1786'

Currently, spread all around was a selection of books. The texts were lined with writing so small that Percy needed three magnifying glasses to read them. This did not stand in Professor Devereux's way, however, as he seemed to know their contents off by heart.

"During the medieval times," he began, "there were many roads. They were usually on the floor and laid in a northerly direction..."

The professor had taken his place in front of a blackboard and was so lost in today's lesson that Percy dared to stop listening. He looked over the professor's shoulder and caught sight of something glinting atop a bookcase.

Behind the blackboard and to the right, Percy could see his botany box. He raised himself ever so slightly on his stool and moved slowly so as not to make a single sound. For all he knew, Grandmother could have her ear trumpet planted firmly on the ground, waiting for any hint of noise.

"...and, further to that, the king decided that his private roads should be built exactly three feet above the ground, which led to the creation of walls..."

The slow scratching of the professor's chalk pierced the dusty air, and Percy sprang on the chance to push his stool back. He stood, took three cautious breaths and waited for either Grandmother or Professor Devereux to respond.

Nothing.

Percy took a few moments to plan his route. He stood behind the grand desk. Professor Devereux was on the far side, facing the blackboard.

As an infant, Percy had spent much time in the library. Mother had believed that, by leaving him to play surrounded by the books, she could help young Percy to absorb the wealth of knowledge within. Whether or not this had worked was unclear but what Percy did have was a good knowledge of which floorboards made which sound. The ones nearest to the bookcases made a *squeal*; the boards supporting the reading desk made a *groan*; the ones hammered with the screws rather than nails made a *shriek*; and those under the carpet were prone to shouting 'OI, GET OFF'. With this in mind, Percy rounded the table and tiptoed between the odd few that made no sound at all.

Professor Devereux continued. "Many skirmishes took place between the two factions: the first believing that roads should be no wider than a horse's front end and the second insistent that the most accurate measurement should be that of a cow's..."

Percy carefully placed one foot and then another onto Grandmother's old reclining chair, which was positioned next to the bookshelf that held his botany box. He had spent so much time jumping from the library ladders onto the chair with Daisy that the springs were broken and poking through the split fabric.

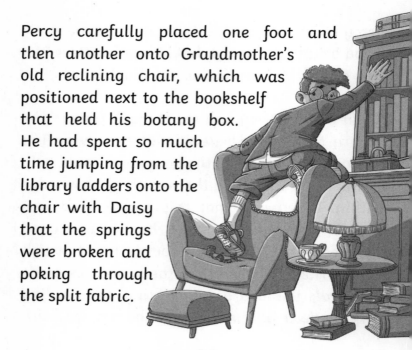

He was so close to the box! The professor was still facing the other way and lost in his teaching flow. If Percy could just lean out a little farther, he might be able to pull it towards him and then... he leant just a little too far.

Grandmother's chair wobbled dangerously and Percy's feet slipped on the soft, velvet fabric. His weight forced the chair to topple over, crashing onto its side and knocking over a side table. Percy landed with a thud, taking a handful of books with him. For a few moments, he lay on the polished, wooden floor, unable to move.

Then, a slow, groaning voice spoke. "What are you doing, Master Percival?"

"I, uh..." Percy took hold of the nearest book and pushed himself up to stand. "I was just so excited by this book, I simply had to read it!"

Professor Devereux's eyes lit up. Percy knew that the professor was passionate about books, no matter the shape, size or content. If there was one thing that could cause the professor's eyes to mist over dreamily, it was the sight of a book – the older, the better.

"How pleasing it is to see you take such an interest in..." Professor Devereux plucked the book from Percy's hands, steadied his monocle and gazed at the leather detail and the name stitched into the spine. "Well, I have not seen this particular text in quite some years."

Percy took the book and headed back to his desk. Ahead of him, Professor Devereux smiled. "I believe that you were meant to find this, Master Percival."

Percy looked down at the leather-bound journal. The cover was so thick that it could have been used to make a pair of wellington boots. The text inside was handwritten and Percy saw fine, detailed drawings of leaves, fruits and flowers, all beautifully labelled. This was a treasure trove of all things botanical, but what amazed Percy most was the name printed on the cover.

Benedict Poll – his grandfather.

# Chapter Four

"Dinner!" Father called at six o'clock sharp as he carefully placed the chipped and cracked crockery onto the large dining table. The table itself had been rescued from a shipwreck off the Spanish coast many generations before. The underside was lined with molluscs and fossilised seaweed. Percy had once asked if they could clean it, but Mother had said that it had belonged to the sea first and that they were merely borrowing it.

When his family did not immediately run to

eat their portion of tonight's meal of rhubarb and mushroom eclairs, Father grew impatient. He turned and walked to the house bells in the scullery. He eyed the series of tasselled cords beneath the dozens of bells. Each was linked to a different area in the house and was Father's most direct way of contacting his family, wherever they may be.

"Hmm..." he mused, stroking his chin. He pulled a much-used cord in the middle of the panel. From somewhere in the attic, he heard a loud and telltale *thud*.

"Now, the children. They surely could be anywhere."

Next, he rang the bell for Daisy's room. The tinkling echo drifted through the house and he smiled. Then, he pulled the cord that connected to Percy's bedroom.

There were a few seconds of silence – and then the cord came away in his hand. Father was forced to take a step backwards as reels of stiff rope slid out of the wall cavity and pooled at his feet. He inspected the frayed rope and carefully felt the end. It was wet with a strange, sticky substance. He held his finger to his nose and sniffed. "How odd..."

He tried a few more bells in order to locate his son but quickly lost patience, so began to ring bells, one and then another and then another, at random. Within seconds, the house was filled with the sound of bells jangling. It would have been the most beautiful music had it not been such chaos. When cracks appeared in the walls and flecks of plaster began to fall from the ceiling, Father decided that he had made his point.

*

"What an absolute racket!" Grandmother muttered to herself as she shuffled slowly down the stairs from her attic room. "It is just noise,

noise, noise in this house. Whatever happened to 'silence is golden' and 'children should be seen and not heard'?"

Grandmother Poll was the oldest, and therefore the most important, member of the Poll family. She had been born in Poll Manor, schooled in Poll Manor, had grown old in Poll Manor and would haunt Poll Manor long after she passed. In her mind, it was her duty to keep her family living up to the high standards that she had set.

She spent her days on the uppermost floor of the house, where she chronicled the life of her canine companion. Bratwurst made a fine model for her portraits and was the closest thing she ever got to intelligent conversation.

40

From the rooms around her, the clanging and jangling of bells continued. She stopped suddenly on the corridor of the second floor by the three suits of armour. One of them now lay scattered in pieces on the floor – but that was not what had caught her eye. On the wall behind where the knight had once stood was an enormous crack, running almost from floor to ceiling. This in itself was not unusual – new cracks were always appearing in the walls of the old house – but as she shuffled closer, she could see a purple liquid oozing from the crack.

"Disgusting!" she remarked to no one in particular. "This house gets more and more run-down every day. Why, when I was a girl, my..." She paused and squinted again at the purplish slime that was seeping out of the wall. "Although," she muttered, "this shade of purple is just the colour I need for Bratwurst's dress." She thought about one of her current works in progress, which she had titled 'A Dachshund in Distress' – a portrait of Bratwurst as Rapunzel in her tower. He had protested greatly at the addition of the wig.

Grandmother took a vase from a small side table

and placed it on the floor next to the weeping wall. A large drop of the liquid ran down the wooden panelling and collected in the bottom of the container. She nodded approvingly and continued on her journey down to the kitchen.

\*

Mother hummed a tune to accompany the tinkling bells as she floated down the first-floor corridor towards Percy's bedroom, a sieve and her container of lemon sherbet under one arm. Although she had left some under his sheets during the morning, she had seen her youngest looking troubled as he had raced around the house earlier and she had decided that he would need *very* sweet dreams that night.

She gently pushed open the heavy, wooden door and entered the room. Oblivious to the covering of leaves that now blanketed the wall next to the bed, she headed instead to check the thermometer in the corner of the room. Happy that the display was still showing a perfect twenty-and-a-quarter degrees Celsius, she continued with her task. Lifting the bedsheets, she poured a sprinkling of sherbet into the sieve and carefully dusted the fine powder over the mattress and underneath the pillows. Satisfied with the job, she smiled serenely and turned to leave.

Just then, her eye caught sight of the three crimson berries that peeked out from underneath the leaves and glittered invitingly. "Oh, how lovely," she murmured to herself, gently plucking them from the stem and placing them carefully into the pocket of her flowing skirt. She knew just the place for them.

\*

In the library, seated back at the desk, Percy could only hear the faintest tinkling when the bells rang. All afternoon, he had been itching to get back to his bedroom and pore over his grandfather's book. He might even be able to classify the strange plant that he had, only a few hours ago, brought home.

"I believe that dinner is ready," Professor Devereux said in the same monotonous tone he had been using all afternoon.

"Thank you, Professor," Percy replied.

"Any time, Master Percival. I do hope you will enjoy reading your grandfather's observations. He was quite the botanist."

Percy's heart fluttered at the thought. "Was he?"

Professor Devereux smiled. "Oh, yes. I taught him everything he knew. I do believe it was somewhat of an obsession."

Percy nodded in silent thanks but was struck with an image of a younger Professor Devereux (if such a thing had ever existed) teaching Grandfather about photosynthesis. He had never heard stories of his grandfather, particularly of when he was young.

"May I step down?"

By the time he had asked the question, however, Professor Devereux had begun to turn his way back round to the blackboard. Usually, this meant that Percy was free to go so he slipped off the stool, passed to the right side of the professor's blackboard and scooped up his botany box from the bookshelf on his way.

"So long, Professor!"

# Chapter Five

As Percy emerged into the corridor, he heard one creak and then another from the floorboards down the hall and round the corner. From the accompanying mumbling and grumbling, he could tell that it was Grandmother on the march.

"Uh-oh!" If Percy were not at his spot at the dinner table when she arrived, there would be trouble. Grandmother, like the professor, had strict rules about punctuality.

Arriving at the kitchen, Percy skidded to a stop. He then walked to the dining table and plonked himself down. He always had the same spot, to the right of the head of the table. Percy looked across the kitchen to his father who was busy dusting his eclairs with gravy granules. Mother was completing the table arrangement with a centrepiece that she had made herself: a woollen fruit bowl, complete with knitted fruit.

"Hello, Petal," Mother said.

"Hello, Mother," Percy replied.

"How were your lessons?" she asked.

Percy took a moment to consider the wonderful discovery he had made. "Most interesting," he said, opening Grandfather's book on his lap. Mother turned away and flitted around the kitchen, moving things from one place to another. Percy did not understand why she did it but she smiled all the while and that was enough.

Carefully, Percy flicked through the detailed drawings and notes in Grandfather's book, looking for anything like his discovery that morning. The book was separated into different sections: features of plants, their functions, healthy habitats, what they needed to survive, life cycles and reproduction.

For a seed to germinate, certain conditions must be met.

Water, oxygen, light, nutrients and a suitable temperature are vital to a plant's survival.

Grandfather Poll had obviously spent a lot of time observing the natural world. As Percy went to read on, the rest of the family began to arrive for dinner. He slipped the book under his chair, on top of his botany box.

One by one, the remaining members of the Poll family took their places at the table. Daisy took a seat next to Percy with Mother opposite. Father (when he stopped stirring pots and pans) would briefly sit next to Mother; however, there was always some other dish he had forgotten or left to burn on the hob.

"Mother," Percy asked, "why doesn't the professor join us for dinner?" It had always seemed odd to Percy that he never saw the professor outside of the library.

"He takes his meals in private," she replied.

"But why?" Percy asked.

Father turned and answered Percy's question. "Let's just say that he and your grandmother don't get on," he explained.

"Talking about me again, Basil?" a fierce, rasping voice called.

Percy turned and watched as his grandmother entered the kitchen. Grandmother's feet made the same swooshing sound as a brush sweeping the kitchen tiles.

"That old blowhard is not welcome at my table!" she continued at top volume.

From Percy's position at the table, he could just see the top of Grandmother's bouffant hair peeking out over the lip of the countertops. When she rounded the corner, her face was so creased into a frown, it looked like it was trying to eat itself.

"What happened between her and the professor?" Percy whispered to his sister, who now sat by his side.

"Mum told me he used the wrong fish fork once."

Percy's mouth fell open. *The wrong fork for fish!* No wonder he was banished.

Looking back to Grandmother, Percy took in the sight of her fine tunic covered in a colourful sarape. Usually, it was men who wore sarapes and this one had belonged to Grandfather. One slow shuffle at a time, Grandmother approached a set of small steps set up by her chair. She took them, one, two and three, finally dragging herself into place at the very head of the table. She observed the family one at a time. Then, she began the daily moan.

"Why are you so dirty?" she barked, eyeing Daisy.

Daisy stopped moving her eclair around the plate with her fork. "Well, Grandmother, I spent most of this afternoon inspecting the pipes on the first floor. For some reason, we aren't able to draw any water from the boiler. At first, I thought it was the paint from your studio clogging up the pipes, but now..."

Grandmother seemed unfazed by what Daisy had just said and merely replied, "My portraits are the only things that make this miserable house a home."

By portraits, Grandmother was referring to her many, many paintings of Bratwurst dressed in various costumes. Percy's personal favourite was the one of him dressed as King Henry VIII – padded tunic and all.

"As a Poll, you should be clean for supper," Grandmother was saying. Before Daisy had a chance to respond, the old woman turned her attention towards Mother. "Must we use this terrible crockery? Where are the plates from

Her Majesty the Queen? They were a gift, you know!" she yelled.

Percy gulped and caught Mother's eye. For many years, she had kept secret the fact that Percy had smashed all those plates while attempting to build a box fort, aged five. Mother had used the same excuse since that day.

"The Queen wishes them to continue to be on display at the palace," she recited, "and you cannot refuse the Queen."

Grandmother huffed but said no more about it. Her next target was Percy, with the usual complaint. "Must you breathe so loudly?" she scoffed, covering her ears to show how offended she was by Percy's noise.

"No, Grandmother. I shall try to do better." Percy made sure then to hold every third breath.

Finally, she looked towards Father. He had just extinguished a tea towel that had been caught under the grill. "I trust you won't be adding that to tomorrow's breakfast? This food is foul; I wouldn't feed it to my dog." This last sentence gave her a moment's pause. "Where *is* my dog? Bratwurst? Bratwurst!" she called, spitting flecks of savoury eclair all over Percy.

Grandmother looked all around, slamming her fists onto the table, knocking over the crystal glass in front of her and spilling the ruby liquid within. She hammered her fists like a toddler in a tantrum, also knocking over Daisy's water, Mother's iced tea and Father's cup of gravy.

"Where is my BRATWURST?" she screeched.

Percy tried to remember the last time he had seen the family dog. It had been that morning, just after he had brought the plant home. Bratwurst had tumbled down the stairs from Grandmother's attic studio and plodded off somewhere he could hide and avoid being put in another costume.

"There!" Grandmother yelled as she pointed towards pairs of tiny, painted paw prints leading to the scullery. That was where the house bells were and also a staircase leading down to the cellar rooms of Poll Manor.

Percy always tried to stay out of the cellar. It was dark, wet and seemed to trigger his allergies. Daisy, however, loved it down there. She would say that down there, among the broken pipes and hungry rodents, was the calmest place in the whole house.

Grandmother, her face now a fierce, red scowl, pushed herself up in her chair. She looked from Daisy, to Percy and then back again. "FIND MY DOG!" she bellowed, her cry almost shattering all the windows in the room.

*

"I tell you what, Petal – if I find that dog, I am going to serve him up with a bowl of mashed potatoes."

Daisy had made her feelings about Grandmother's sausage dog very clear on many occasions. On the long list of things that Daisy disliked about Bratwurst, his ability to get into Poll Manor's nooks and crannies was number one, two and three.

"I mean, you tell me how a dog that round

can fit through a loose floorboard or a hole in the wall."

"I suppose it depends on the size of the hole," Percy remarked as he wandered along by his sister's side. Grandmother had demanded that they go into the cellar to look for Bratwurst. Both Percy and Daisy knew not to argue with her. For someone who disliked noise as much as Grandmother, she certainly was able to make a lot of it when she needed to.

Daisy led the way down the creaky stairs. She pulled the ancient string for the light but the bulb blew out as she did and they were plunged into total darkness. It didn't last long, however, as Daisy always seemed to have the correct equipment somewhere on a belt, in a bag or tucked up her jumper. She handed Percy an electric torch and took one for herself.

"I think he must have gone this way," Percy said. He pointed his torch downwards, illuminating the last traces of yellow paint that stained the concrete. The damp, dewy floor must have disturbed and moistened the last of Grandmother's paint that had clung to

Bratwurst's paws.

The cellar under Poll Manor consisted of a main room, which the stairs led down into. Half a dozen small, brick rooms came off this one. Percy had no idea, and really didn't want to know, what they held inside them. The cellar was Daisy's problem. He could hear the clattering and clanging of the boiler coming from the room at the end.

Percy let his torchlight follow the faint patches of yellow towards one of the many doors that came off the main cellar. His beam showed him that the rickety, wooden door to the room was slightly ajar. "I think he went in here," he called to Daisy, stepping carefully to avoid the pools of water on the floor.

"Great!" said Daisy. She had found a dripping pipe and was pulling out her spanner to tighten the loose nut. "You go and grab the little dumpling and I'll check on the boiler while I'm here."

Percy pushed open the slightly battered door and was met by the fiercely musty smell of stale water. The air was so thick with damp that Percy could almost taste it. He scanned the room with his torch, taking in the sight of old storage boxes that were thick with rot. As he stepped through the doorway, the floor changed from stone slabs to dirty, wooden boards. He spotted an oblong shape squeezing itself through a small hole in the wall on the far side of the room.

Percy rushed in to try to grab Bratwurst before his last, stumpy paw disappeared, but he missed. He stood, raising his torch, and inspected the small hole. It really did amaze him how flexible that dog could be.

He was just about to kneel down to see where the hole might lead to when he heard his sister's voice behind him.

"Uh, Percy... I think you should come and see this."

Percy turned and saw Daisy standing in the doorway. He followed her out of the small room and back into the main cellar. Percy could hear the clanking of the old boiler... and something else. It was a regular, rhythmic whooshing, like a sleeping dragon's breath.

Daisy stood beside the thinly framed door to the boiler room and waited for him to open it. As he approached, the noise grew louder. Cautiously, Percy put his hand on the door and pushed it open.

"Oh my!"

# Chapter Six

The ancient, cast iron boiler was the beating heart of Poll Manor. At the very bottom, coal was shovelled in and this heated the huge tank of water which sat above. Thick, copper pipes formed veins and arteries that ran along the walls, under the floors and across the ceilings of the great house. From Grandmother's attic to Father's kitchen and everything in-between, the boiler served each family member's unique and varied needs.

Percy passed the beam of his torch over the

61

scene in front of him. The walls, the floor and the huge boiler itself were covered by a blanket of green tendrils. Roots had attached themselves onto everything in sight, crawling over every surface and inching towards the leaking pipes of the boiler and the pools of water that had formed underneath.

When Percy had scooped up the tiny plant and placed it in the jam jar that morning, it had wilted. It had needed something to keep it alive. Percy squinted at one of the slithering roots and realised why Daisy had been having so much trouble with the leaking pipes and clunky plumbing. The plant's roots had found the largest water source in the house and had latched onto it.

Looking up to the ceiling, he could see the roots beginning to turn into a thick, green stem. The plant had expanded downwards from Percy's bedroom and was now growing inside the walls.

"What do you think it is?" Daisy asked. As she spoke, the roots of the plant seemed to flinch and the air turned still. It felt as though the plant were listening.

"Ssh!" Percy whispered. "I think it's attracted to noise." He looked at his sister and the hard frown on her face. "We should get out of here. Back up slowly." Percy was not used to telling Daisy what to do but he knew more about this kind of thing than she did, and she seemed to be thinking along the same lines.

"Good idea. Grandmother will have to find her precious pudding herself," she said.

Percy ran back to the empty kitchen with Daisy by his side. He scooped up their grandfather's book as well as his botany box and they managed to escape up to Percy's bedroom just before Father came back to the kitchen to begin mashing blue cheese for the next day's breakfast smoothies.

*

The walls of Percy's bedroom were now completely covered by a web of leaves. Attracted to the light that poured in throughout the day from his huge windows, the leaves had flourished. Now, however, the sun was setting and, at this time of day, everything the light

63

touched looked baked in marmalade. The purple leaves had begun to curl in on themselves and the plant almost seemed as if it were sleeping.

"It's nyctinastic," Percy announced breathlessly, as the pair stood in the doorway taking in the view of the bedroom. "It closes in the dark."

"At least it won't grow any more overnight, then," Daisy replied.

Percy set the book and botany box on top of his bed.

"What's that?" Daisy asked.

"It's from Grandfather. It might help us to understand what this plant is. I haven't seen anything like it before but maybe Grandfather did."

"It's just a weed," Daisy said.

"Yeah, but did you see the way it reacted to you? It's in the walls, Daisy. We need to get rid of it now."

"You're the one who brought it inside!" she retorted.

Percy frowned and curled his lip, eyeing his mother's thermometer in the corner of the room. "It's still growing. If it keeps going at this rate tomorrow, it's going to bring the whole house down!"

"I hate to tell you this, Petal, but this house has been falling down for the last fifty years. I'll have to use your garden shears to get the roots out of the boiler in the morning. First, sprout pudding and now this," she tutted. "It's a wonder we've got any hot water at all!"

Once Daisy had left, Percy sat on his bed and considered what they had found in the cellar and the jungle of leaves that now covered his bedroom walls. The plant had grown at an enormous rate since he had discovered it this morning. He thought about how it had begun to wilt in the jar and yet, as soon as he opened the lid, it had buried itself in his bedroom wall and seemed to take on a life of its own.

Blinking away the warm glow of the setting sun,

Percy lay down and set his grandfather's book on his chest. The heavy journal opened with a creak. Like Professor Devereux's old, croaky bones, Grandfather's book awoke from a long and restless sleep. The first few pages still held on to that sweet and musty smell that lingered in Percy's nose.

Carefully, he eased each page aside, making sure not to tear and crumple any of the precious words. He was desperately seeking something that resembled the plant which was rapidly becoming part of the house. Soon, however, absolutely exhausted from the events of the day, he felt his eyes becoming heavy and he drifted off into a sleep full of sweet dreams, just as Mother had intended.

\*

"Morning, Petal. Rise and shine!"

Percy opened his eyes to see his sister entering his bedroom. Sitting up, he rubbed his face and picked up his glasses, which had fallen onto the bed during the night. As he did so, his face brushed against the mass of leaves that were clinging to the bedroom wall.

Daisy walked over and sat down heavily at the edge of Percy's bed. Small clouds of lemon sherbet wafted out from under the mattress.

"Did you manage to find anything about this?" She gestured to the patchwork of leaves that covered Percy's walls.

As the morning light streamed in through his windows, Percy noticed that the plant's leaves had unfurled once more and were gently turning towards the light. Percy knew that his bedroom, with its enormous windows, was the ideal environment for the leaves to absorb the light and photosynthesise using the chlorophyll inside the cells.

"Not yet," Percy replied. Once again, he carefully opened the journal, angling it so that Daisy could also see. Together, they entered their grandfather's world of plants, petals and peculiar things.

As they fluttered through the pages, Percy saw a wondrous story of the natural world emerge.

# Percy Poll's Peculiar Plants

His grandfather, Benedict Poll, had drawn the most detailed illustrations of the plants of Poll Manor. Not only had he documented the gardens – he had designed them.

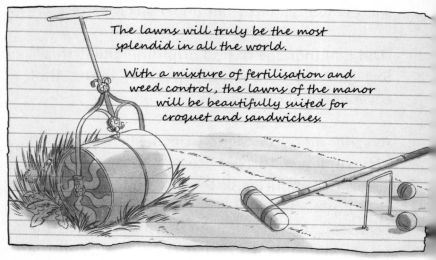

The lawns will truly be the most splendid in all the world.

With a mixture of fertilisation and weed control, the lawns of the manor will be beautifully suited for croquet and sandwiches.

They went on to read a section about flowers.

Flowerbeds must be formal, including a variety of colours, heights and arrangements.

Gertrude Jekyll may claim a different approach, yet I remain unconvinced.

Echinacea

Dalia

Boraginaceae

Antirrhinum

Gertrude Jekyll! The Victorian horticulturalist had known almost everything there was to know about plants in their grandfather's time. Had they been friends?

Percy and Daisy continued to flick through the pages, scanning them for anything that looked like their plant. Perhaps it had been an invasive species and never crossed his grandfather's path.

Nothing. Percy slammed the book down onto the bed in frustration.

"Don't worry, Petal. Nothing ever got fixed by reading a book."

Just as Daisy said these words, a small scrap of paper slipped out of the open book that now lay on top of the eiderdown. Percy leant forwards and picked up the scrap. The parchment was old and crinkled. He turned it over in his hands and observed the hastily drawn sketches and notes.

It was his plant! Percy opened his botany box and removed the magnifying glass. Underneath the glass, Percy was able to make out the drawing of the weed.

"Is that it?" asked Daisy.

Percy studied the sketch, recognising the dark berries and thorny leaves. In his grandfather's picture, it looked like the plant was outside in its natural environment. Percy could see various scribblings around the plant that labelled its parts. There were also a few paragraphs detailing everything his grandfather had learnt.

First was its scientific name: *Asteraceae psychivorum*. Percy knew that the first word, Asteraceae, meant that it belonged to a large family of flowering plants, but the second one was new.

"Psychivorum?" Percy wondered aloud.

Below this, his grandfather had written a few short sentences.

The psychivorum thrives in the usual way through adequate light, air and water, yet there is another quality that makes it bloom. The psychivorum requires a certain type of nutrient quite unlike any other plant.

Percy gulped as he read Grandfather's final words.

This plant feeds on
human thoughts.

Treat with extreme caution
and avoid contact at all
costs — and whatever you do,
don't let it inside the house!

# Chapter Seven

Throughout his life, Percy had studied many different flora and fauna. Poll Manor attracted all types of weird and wonderful plants and creatures. The family had long since let nature take over and the once-landscaped gardens had grown wild.

With his trusty botany box in hand, Percy had found out interesting facts about almost all of his favourite plants. He had counted over fourteen varieties of delphiniums in the manor grounds but knew from his reading in the library that there were actually over four hundred in the world. He knew that to make a peony bush grow strong, it needed potassium. It amazed him to know how hollyhocks had been used in medicine throughout time.

Plants were a reflection of their environment. The hydrangeas, for example, would change colour based on the soil. If it was acidic, they would turn blue. If it was alkaline, they would bloom in pink.

Percy was continually fascinated by plants. They seemed almost to have their own desires, be able to make their own choices, friends, even enemies – but, in all his studies, he had never seen anything quite like the psychivorum. Percy had learnt that the natural world was filled with incredible species that had evolved to survive in very specific situations, but he had never heard of a plant that could feed off human thoughts before. Was it possible? What he did know was that they were all in danger and he needed to put a stop to this plant's growth before it consumed the thoughts of anyone in his family.

"We should tell Mother," Percy said.

"Why? She's probably busy rotating the pillows at three miles per hour."

"She'll know what to do," Percy insisted. "She always knows where everything is meant to go."

"If you say so..." Daisy raised an eyebrow and shot Percy a half-smile that told him she wasn't convinced he was right but she didn't have a better idea.

Percy and Daisy set out on a quest to find their mother. She had always been there to listen and would be able to help – Percy just knew it. As they walked through the kitchen, they were drawn to the scullery by a clattering and clanging that could only belong to one person.

"Hi, Dad," Daisy said, pushing open the door. The scullery was a small side room just off the kitchen. It had a table in the centre and two of the four walls were lined with deep, oak shelves dotted with woodworm. On the shelves were wooden boxes full of food and glass jars of pickles, jams and spreads, as well as flours and grains of all descriptions. It amazed Percy how Father managed to turn all these wonderful ingredients into such truly, truly awful food.

Inside the room, Father was all a flutter, lifting, shifting and sometimes dropping boxes of jams, pickles and preserves that had been left on the floor.

"Father!" Percy called, bursting past his sister and into the room. Daisy strolled in a few seconds after him.

"Ah, hello, Petal," he replied, placing a wooden box full of parsnip marmalade onto a low shelf. "Hello, Flower," he added, smiling at Daisy.

Percy took a moment, turned to his sister and realised it had been a long time since he had heard anyone use Daisy's nickname. He made a mental note to bring it back into everyday use.

He turned back to his father. "Something is wrong. Have you seen Mother?"

"The only thing that's wrong is your mother moving my ingredients," he said, breezing a hand over the stacks of boxes. "I can't tell my swedes from my sultanas, my figs from my flan and there are mice everywhere!"

"Pardon?" Percy said.

Daisy approached and loomed over Percy's shoulder. She looked across the boxes and the particular way Mother had arranged them.

"Mice," Father repeated. He gestured towards her rows of boxes that created a small valley from one hole in the wall to another hole on another wall. "She made them a road to get into the garden, except that most of them hang around eating my ingredients!"

"At least someone is," Daisy muttered under her breath.

Percy took his father's sleeve and tugged it. "Where is Mother?"

"I believe she's still in bed. She wasn't feeling too bright this morning. Now, away with you, children. I need to prepare breakfast and have a strong word with a rat about my ravioli."

He turned back to rearranging his jars.

Shrugging, Daisy walked out of the scullery and into the main kitchen. Percy followed his sister past the large, antique dining table that still contained plates piled high with the remains of last night's offerings. Percy knew that Mother liked to leave the dishes out overnight to allow the mice to have a midnight feast if they so desired.

In the middle of the table was Mother's centrepiece – the knitted fruit bowl that she had arranged so carefully last night. Something inside it was glinting in the morning sun.

Percy walked over to take a closer look and gasped as he realised what it was. Nestled between the woollen banana and knitted pear were three dark red spheres.

The berries. Mother had touched them.

Percy's heartbeat suddenly began to thud in his ears. Catching up with Daisy, he grabbed her by the wrist and pulled. "We've got to get to Mother now!"

*

Percy and Daisy ran the final few steps to Mother and Father's bedroom on the second floor. The door stood barely open and there was no sound coming from within. Percy was scared of what they might discover on the other side.

"There's nothing to worry about, Petal," Daisy said reassuringly from behind him.

Percy stepped forwards and gently pushed open the door to his parents' bedroom. When his eyes fell upon the scene inside, his breath caught in his throat.

It was vaguely possible to spot Mother lying on the bed against the back wall of the bedroom but she was too far away to see clearly. Between her and the doorway, the room had been turned upside down in a frenzy. The psychivorum seemed to have broken through the walls in dozens of places and the air in front of Percy was filled with tangled, fibrous vines, which were prowling slowly around the space like eels in a tank.

"Percy," Daisy murmured uncertainly. At the sound of her voice, each tendril stopped still and

twisted its tip towards the door. Daisy quickly covered her mouth with her hand as the image of Mother that they could see through the gaps was swallowed up by a writhing mass of long, powerful-looking vines, each one quivering curiously like the nose of a hunting dog.

There was no way that they would be able to reach Mother while the plant was guarding her like this. Percy grabbed his sister's hand in his own, took the doorknob in his other hand and eased it closed, backing out of the room with his eyes fixed on the psychivorum's many outstretched fingertips.

# Chapter Eight

Percy's heart thumped against his chest as he and Daisy hurried along the corridors of Poll Manor. The pair needed the help of someone with a wise head on their shoulders if they were going to rescue Mother. Unfortunately, wisdom was in short supply within the walls of the crumbly, old house. With their grandfather's book and the botany box in hand, Percy and Daisy headed to the most secluded place in the whole house – Professor Devereux's living quarters, where he ate and slept.

Travelling along the second-floor corridor towards the west wing, every step brought to their attention more damage to Poll Manor's walls and furniture. The old cracks in the panelled walls seemed to be widening and oozing with a strange, purple sap; the carpets looked as though they were straining at the seams and the walls seemed almost to be alive.

"I still don't understand how the professor could possibly help us," Daisy was saying.

Percy turned to her. "The professor told me that he taught Grandfather everything he knew, which means he must have been around when Grandfather first encountered the psychivorum. If anyone knows what has happened and how to fix it, it will be him."

"I've been doing so well at avoiding the professor," Daisy moaned. "I haven't been to a trombone lesson in three weeks."

Percy did not respond.

"I used the wretched instrument to fix the U-bend in the downstairs bathroom," she continued as they reached the door to Professor Devereux's living quarters.

Percy knocked.

For a few moments, there was no sound at all. As far as Percy could remember, no one in their family ever came to this part of the house and Professor Devereux only left to go to the library to teach him about ancient roads, types of chairs and the long and interesting history of the baguette.

Daisy sighed. What's taking so –"

"Shh!" Percy said. "I can hear something."

Percy heard locks, buzzers and the unlatching of a security chain. He watched as the door handle slowly began to turn and the door creaked open. Percy was not sure what he had expected, seeing Professor Devereux at this early hour in his private quarters. He had never been inside this room before and was picturing all sorts of things, like the old man dressed in extravagant pyjamas or sealed inside a giant mechanical pod to keep him young. Instead, when he opened the door, the professor was in his wheelchair, as usual, wearing a full three-piece suit and crooked bow tie, his monocle almost lost in the wrinkles of his face.

"Master Percival. Miss Daisy. You have no lessons this morning."

"I am sorry to disturb you, Professor, but we have a problem that we need help with."

"This is most irregular," the professor replied, reaching to close the door. "Perhaps it could wait until this afternoon."

Daisy held up Grandfather's book, catching the professor's attention. "It's to do with a book!"

The professor's eyes suddenly sparkled. He looked from Daisy, to Percy and then back again before saying, "In that case, you had better come in."

Stepping into Professor Devereux's living quarters felt like stepping into his brain. It was much smaller than the library, where they had their daily lessons; to their left was Professor Devereux's desk with two red wingback chairs in front of it. At the far end, opposite, there was a large, glass vivarium that housed a bearded dragon, which was almost completely camouflaged by the foliage inside the tank.

The rest of the room was littered with the strangest objects and inventions. Mounted on the right-hand wall, Percy saw an ancient, carved cannon and what looked like the wooden wheel of an old ship. The most unusual object, though, was the professor's prized possession: a suit of Japanese armour that stood beside his desk. The karuta armour was made of rectangular tiles and had a katana, a curved, single-edged blade, at its hip.

The professor pushed a button on the right-hand side of his wheelchair. Suddenly, the wheels engaged and he began to approach his desk slowly. As he did, Percy and Daisy walked to the red, leather seats and sat down.

From the other side of the desk, Professor Devereux spoke. "Now, then. What have you found inside your grandfather's book?"

Percy knew that he could trust the professor.

He was as old as the walls of Poll Manor. He had seen generations of change and a walking, thought-consuming plant may just be the kind of subject in which he was an expert.

Percy placed not only the book but the slip of paper down in front of him on the desk. The professor twisted and turned his monocle, smacked his lips together and made a range of 'ooh', 'aah' and 'umm' sounds. Beside Percy, Daisy's knees were bouncing up and down impatiently. Everything the professor did seemed to take a very long time and Daisy lived her life at ten times his speed.

"Yes, yes... I do remember this specimen. Your grandfather was a mere boy – not much older than you, I do believe."

"And what happened?" Daisy asked immediately.

The professor scowled at her from underneath his bushy eyebrows. "Well, he grew up, of course, Miss Daisy! I should think that would be obvious."

"Not to Grandfather – to the plant!" Daisy cried.

"Ah. Yes. Right. Well, the plant that he describes in this text was quite the little thing, I must say. I remember that it was disturbing the hydrangeas for a short time."

*The hydrangeas?* thought Percy. That didn't sound like the colossal, rapid-growing and threatening weed that was taking over the manor.

"And did it ever..." Percy swallowed as a guilty lump formed in the back of his throat. "Did it ever find its way into the house, Professor?"

The old man looked surprised. "Into the house? No, I shouldn't think so. As I recall, young Master Benedict spent much – no, almost all – of his time in the gardens," the professor said fondly. "Oh, yes. He was always clipping this and potting that. In fact," he continued, turning his chair to face out of the tall window, "I do believe that if you were to look from any window in the manor, you would be able to spot some of his handiwork. He was very particular about the size and shape of the borders, you see. In fact, in one of our algebra lessons..."

The professor launched into a long and rambling story, gesturing energetically. Losing interest, Percy stood and began to pace around the room. He felt angry with himself. Grandfather had known better than to bring an unfamiliar plant into Poll Manor. Left alone outside with no thoughts to feed on, the psychivorum had probably stayed a very normal, non-terrifying size. Now, it had taken his mother and it was all his fault. He felt like crying – but they didn't have time for that.

After a minute or two of furious thinking, Percy turned his attention once more to the

vivarium that housed the professor's pet. Although bearded dragons were typically found in the rocky deserts of Australia, the vivarium's carefully controlled environment made sure that the conditions were just right for the reptile. Being cold-blooded, bearded dragons relied on a heat source, such as the sun, to raise their body temperature, so the creature needed a heat lamp on one side of its tank and a special fluorescent light. Live insects were also hopping around the glass case and these, along with an assortment of fruit and vegetables, provided the reptile with the right nutrients.

As the professor droned on about calculating the length of the perfect lawn border, Percy considered how plants also needed a carefully controlled environment in order to survive.

"Daisy," he wondered aloud, "if I wanted to remove all the water from the boiler, could I? Is it possible to dry out the cellar completely?" He was staring at the small water fountain in the bottom of the lizard's tank which kept it hydrated.

Across the room, Daisy chuckled. "What? Remove all the water from the house? You'd cause a riot! Grandmother would want her boiling hot bath, and what would Father use to steam his ice cream ravioli? Actually," she said, rolling her eyes, "don't answer that."

"But if we wanted to," Percy pressed her, "could we?"

His sister shook her head apologetically. "Sorry, Petal. That boiler pumps and filters water directly from the lake. Even if I shut it off, it'd take ages to empty it altogether and you'd never get that cellar completely dry."

Percy's heart sank. He thought hard about each of the things that the psychivorum needed to survive but couldn't think of a way to remove any of them. He ran his long fingers through his hair and sighed heavily.

Over at the desk, Daisy stood and pushed her chair back with a long and piercing screech. "Let's go," she said. She collected Grandfather's book and the botany box off the desk, before walking over to Percy at the glass tank and placing a hand on his shoulder. "Come on. We can find another way to help Mother," she reassured him gently – but she didn't sound convinced.

"Thank you, Professor," Percy said as they turned to leave.

The professor was still lecturing to thin air about the history of the manor's gardens. With a jerk as though waking from a dream, he turned and called, "Oh, Master Percival, Miss Daisy. Are you leaving?"

They looked back at him. "Yes, Professor," replied Percy wearily, "unless you can think of anything else unusual that took place in that same year."

The professor stroked his beard. "I'm sorry, young master. It was a fine year for the gardens. Everything was in full bloom and even the kraken in the lake came to the surface to enjoy the pleasant weather..."

Daisy rolled her eyes. Percy sighed and turned once more to leave.

"...which was quite a relief, I can tell you, after the previous summer. Just one year earlier, the sun had been high and hot – terribly hot – and the gardens just could not cope. Brittle, brown things they became in the heat. It upset young Master Benedict quite regularly."

"Well, that doesn't make sense," said Daisy bluntly. "Plants like warmth, Petal. You told me so yesterday."

Percy stopped in his tracks. Staring into the middle distance, he quietly repeated the professor's words to himself twice over. "Too much," he muttered.

"Petal?"

# Chapter Nine

"There was too much of it!" Percy yelled. He felt as though a firework had gone off somewhere inside him. Grasping Daisy's arm, he steered her towards the exit and through the door, calling over his shoulder, "Thanks, Professor! That was an excellent lesson!" as he closed it behind them.

The professor sat frozen for a few moments, startled. No one had ever complimented his lessons before. It was an unfamiliar but pleasant experience. Straightening his bow tie, the old man sat up a little taller and smirked proudly to himself. After all these years, he had finally got through to a student.

He wheeled over to the door and reattached the security chain. It was almost lunchtime and he still had the afternoon's lessons on medieval pavements to plan. As he pulled his chair back towards the desk, however, a sound drifted across the room. It was a clunking, grinding sound, like that of a cog with something caught in its teeth. Following the sound, the professor found himself in front of a large, metal hatch set into the wall.

This hatch was known as a dumbwaiter, so named after its ability to carry food but its inability to speak. Its function was simple: to transport the professor's meals up to his living quarters from the kitchen, where all Father had to do was place a full plate into the ground-floor hatch and pull a lever. The machine worked much like a miniature elevator.

Now, however, the machine was making sounds that the professor had never heard before. Curiously, he reached out to grasp the handle and pulled open the hatch, half expecting to see yet another marvellous concoction from the family chef. Instead, the entire space inside the wall seemed to be blocked up.

"By Jupiter..." murmured Professor Devereux, turning his monocle with one hand, the better to inspect the situation.

Something was growing inside the wall – there was no doubt about it. A single, thick stem seemed to begin somewhere far below, continue upwards and disappear into the space above the limits of the professor's vision. He craned his neck to peer into the depths of the metal shaft and saw that the stem was dotted with several nodes where offshoots of the plant grew outwards into other rooms.

Suddenly, the professor was thrown backwards as a long, twisting, purple arm shot out of the hatch.

"An invasion!" he cried, pointing his cane at the intruder. "I'll not stand for that type of behaviour. Cease and desist at once. Stop, I say!"

The violently swinging branch roamed around

the professor's living quarters, toppling his wingback chairs and flinging paperwork in all directions. When it came dangerously close to the large display case which housed his precious karuta armour, the professor frowned, threw his cane to one side and rolled up his sleeves.

"Very well," he said. "Then let slip the dogs of war!"

*

Their visit to the professor had been very productive. It had never occurred to Percy that the psychivorum was using the house and the people within it in the same way that he did. To the Poll family, the house provided shelter, food, love, safety and everything else they needed – and it seemed that the house was also providing all the things that the plant needed to thrive. There was no way that they could all share the house's resources, however, and, unfortunately for the psychivorum, the Poll family had been here first.

Percy's mind was working overtime. He thought of Mother trapped behind the psychivorum's vines and felt that the time to save her was slipping away like sand trickling through his fingers.

He knew that plants needed just the right amount of water, light, air, nutrients and warmth to grow well but, from what the professor had told them, too much of these could be almost as bad as too little. It stood to reason that if, in Grandfather's time, too much heat had once damaged the gardens, then now, too much water might make the cellar a poor habitat for the psychivorum.

"Here's what we need to do," Percy said to his sister once they were back in the second-floor corridor. "If it needs water, we'll give it all the water in the world. We're going to flood the cellar."

"The cellar is one heavy rainfall away from flooding most days, anyway," Daisy replied. "But how will that get rid of the plant?"

"We need to give it too much or too little of the things it needs to survive. We can't take away its water so we'll flood it, instead. Then, all we need to do is take away its light, oxygen and..." he paused, "and its nutrients." He wasn't ready to acknowledge that the psychivorum was using their mother as food.

"It all sounds very complicated, Petal," Daisy remarked. "It's just a weed. Surely, we can just chop it down?"

"You can't just trim a weed," Percy replied patiently. "You would have to pull it out completely and it's growing too fast for that." Percy pointed to a thin, green tendril that was now protruding out of a crack in the wall and slithering down the wooden panelling.

"Are you sure?" Daisy fumbled about in her toolbelt. Locating a pair of pliers, she grabbed the vine in her fist and snipped it in two. "See?" she said, throwing the dangling end of the tendril to the floor. "It might take a while but there have been worse things in the walls of this house, let me tell you!"

As the pair continued to walk along the second-floor corridor, a faint *tap, tap, tapping* seemed to come from outside the walls.

"I didn't think it was supposed to rain today," Daisy remarked. No sooner had she said these words than the faint tapping turned into a thumping that sounded like fists hammering against the bricks.

All of a sudden, huge tears split the crimson wallpaper and tore chunks out of the plaster.

The psychivorum was on the move. Defending itself against Daisy's attack, it split the ceiling and its vines and long tendrils sprawled out from the crack, just like they had in Mother and Father's bedroom. For the few seconds that Percy was frozen with fear, the vines crawled their way closer and closer towards him. With the hungry vines less than an arm's length away, Daisy barged into Percy, throwing the two of them onto the floor and out of harm's way.

"Wow!" Percy managed to wheeze as he lay under the weight of his sister.

Daisy pushed herself up off the ground in one swift movement, like an acrobat in greasy dungarees. She reached out her hand and shouted, "Come with me or you'll be plant food!"

Percy grabbed her hand and she pulled him up with such force that he nearly flew through the opposite wall. "Let's go!"

They ran. Every few paces, Percy dared to look over his shoulder. The psychivorum was tearing along the corridor after them. What must have been a dozen separate vines twirled and spiralled like corkscrews, ripping carpets to shreds, smashing sideboards into matchsticks and pulling portraits off the walls like they were made of tissue paper.

"Keep moving!" Daisy cried.

Suddenly, a noise cut through the crashing and a small, squat shape caught Percy's eye.

"Woof!"

"Bratwurst!" Percy called. He looked at the oblong dachshund standing in the doorway of the staircase that led up to Grandmother's attic. Clearly, she had managed to find him again, as he was now wearing a blue and white sailor suit.

"Follow that dog!" Percy yelled. Daisy made a quick dash for the staircase. Percy, a few paces behind, leapt into the safety of the stairwell as the psychivorum lashed out with one great vine, swiping down and missing by a hair's width.

Daisy grabbed the door and slammed it shut. With one great heave, she pulled the heavy, iron bolt across.

"Close one," Percy said, looking up at his sister.

"Yeah, too close," she agreed. They both fell silent as they listened to the psychivorum's strikes thud against the thick, heavy door. After seconds that seemed to last for an eternity, the noise fell away and silence returned.

"Let's go and find Grandmother," Daisy suggested, looking down at Bratwurst. "Where is she, boy? Where's Grandmother?"

Together, Percy, Daisy and Bratwurst ran up the stairs through the rooms leading to Grandmother's studio. They passed through her portrait room, where every possible bit of wall, floor and ceiling space was covered with another painting of Bratwurst. Percy felt a sense of guilt as he accidentally put a foot through a picture of the dachshund dressed as a hotdog.

Next, they made their way through their grandmother's sewing and costume area. Bratwurst clearly did not like that area one bit, as he woofed and snarled all the way through.

Finally, they skidded into Grandmother's studio. Bratwurst had gathered up quite the head of steam and he could not prevent himself from tumbling over and colliding with a short-legged table holding several bottles of paint. When he emerged and shook himself off, a shower of paint speckled the floor, the sofa, the walls and the windows.

"Look what you've done," a dry, crackling voice said. From a corner shrouded in darkness, Grandmother appeared. She was still wearing her grey nightdress with yellow flowers and her hair was tied up in a bun.

"Sorry, Grandmother. It was Bratwurst, really," Percy mumbled.

"Don't you blame him!" Grandmother scolded. "He's a very good boy." Percy watched as Bratwurst latched his teeth onto a red pom-pom attached to the front of a pint-sized clown costume and tore it to confetti. "You're just a menace," Grandmother continued. At that moment, she appeared to notice Daisy for the first time. "Make that two menaces!"

"Grandmother, there's a plant on the loose in the manor –"

"Mess!" Grandmother interrupted, busying herself with picking up the bits and pieces that Bratwurst had knocked over. "That's all that has become of this house." She took one of the old cloth rags she used for wiping her paintbrushes and began to clean the windows, the tables and everywhere else that there was a slick of paint.

"The plant is destroying the house –" Percy tried, but Grandmother continued.

"Once, this manor was the finest in all the land. Now, it is nothing but a crumbling ruin."

Daisy stepped forwards. "If you can't help us,

we are all going to be a crumbling ruin. The psychivorum is down those stairs and we need a plan."

Percy and Daisy both looked on as their grandmother continued to ignore them. She was attempting to clean up the spilt paint. "Just look at this! This will not do. No light at all will get through these windows, now. Although, at least that means I can sleep in and save myself the torture of your father's breakfasts."

Percy watched on as she tried, and failed, to clean the wooden sideboards and the glass. In fact, with every wipe, the greasy oil paint smeared itself more over everything. Then, he felt an idea forming in his mind. Like a splash of paint on a canvas, at first, it was nothing at all. Then, with each passing second, each movement or thought, it took shape.

"Of course!" he whispered to himself.

Grandmother stopped. "What have I told you about breathing loudly?" she snapped.

"Grandmother," Percy said slowly. "The plant

has Mother. It's made her very ill and we need your help."

This seemed to get her attention. For all her tutting and nagging and particularities, Grandmother cared very much about her family.

Percy continued. "This is what we need to do."

# Chapter Ten

The Poll children waited until they were absolutely, one hundred per cent certain that the psychivorum had retreated. Daisy very carefully pulled open the door leading from Grandmother's attic out into the corridor. It was very heavy, as Grandmother had long since soundproofed it with some of Father's hard-setting turnip frosting.

"Let's go," she said. She stepped cautiously onto the carpet hallway runner with Percy behind her and Bratwurst at his side. Grandmother had announced that she needed to change into one of her many 'painting outfits' and then she would join them.

In Percy and Daisy's hands were as many tins of Grandmother's darkest, slimiest oil paint as they could carry. Every tin was black, as it was left over from the time when Grandmother had wanted to paint all her portraits under cover of darkness.

"Are you sure that this is going to work?" Daisy asked, easing the lid off her tin.

"No," Percy admitted, popping the lid off his pot, spilling some onto the fine, antique carpet below, "but it'll be fun."

For a brief moment, Percy and Daisy seemed to forget about the menace tearing apart their home and shared a smile.

With a great heave, Percy turned to the nearest window and launched the contents of his tin towards it. A thick slick of black slime hit the windowpane and splashed off in all directions, hitting the curtain, the carpet, the portraits and the antique candlesticks. Percy couldn't help but let out a squeal of pleasure.

He looked at Daisy, who stood open-mouthed with the brightest eyes he had ever seen. For as long as Percy could remember, Daisy had spent her life keeping things together – now, it was time to let loose.

"Go for it!" he shouted, and so she did. Together, they moved through the corridor, slathering thick, black paint onto the windows. They took extra care to be as messy as possible.

They were so pleased with their plan, in fact, that they decided to paint their clothes, their hair and their faces, too. Daisy drew two pairs of lines across her cheeks to make her look like a fierce warrior. Percy drew a black spot on his nose and a few thin lines on either cheek to look like a cat.

After a few glorious minutes, Percy looked around the darkened corridor, the morning light almost entirely blocked out by the paint, and realised that there was something wrong.

"That ought to stop the psychivorum here but we need to go where its leaves are. The chloroplasts will be absorbing the sun for photosynthesis."

"Cool, cool," Daisy said. "That's all really interesting. I just want to know where I can throw some more paint!"

\*

Standing outside his own bedroom, now with Daisy, Grandmother and Bratwurst in tow, Percy pressed his ear lightly against the wood, trying to listen for movement on the other side. All he could hear was a faint *swish, swish, swish* of something moving beyond. Since he had brought the plant inside, it seemed like there was a surprise waiting for him behind every door. He knew he had to face this surprise head-on, though – his mother was depending on him. Taking a deep breath and reaching the end of a silent countdown, Percy threw open the door.

Inside, his bedroom was now a rippling tide of green and purple. Dozens of leaves grew as offshoots from a thick stem of the psychivorum.

It had smashed through the floorboards, tearing Percy's bed in two. The leaves were pressing themselves hungrily against the wide windows which overlooked the gardens and lake, soaking up as much golden sunlight as they could.

They asked Grandmother to carry on their work, painting the windows of Percy's bedroom first and then the rest of Poll Manor, to make sure no more leaves could absorb the light they needed. She had not shown any interest in the science behind the plan, simply replying, "This house has been crying out for my artistic vision for many years."

"Be careful, Grandmother," Percy warned her. "There's a good chance that the plant will try to defend itself." He thought back to when Daisy had tried to cut one of the vines in the corridor and how the plant had launched an attack on them.

"Don't you worry about me," Grandmother replied. She seemed to have found the energy of someone fifty years younger and was sloshing the paint all over Percy's enormous windows. Almost instantly, the room began to darken.

"Bratwurst will make sure nothing happens to me. Won't you, my little poppet?" Bratwurst woofed and began to flick paint onto the windows with his stubby tail as if to say, "Finally, a paint project I can get on board with!"

Daisy rubbed her dirty hands on her dungarees and turned to Percy. He was pointing to the leaves of the psychivorum, which had now stopped moving and, in some cases, were already beginning to yellow.

"Everything with this plant happens so quickly!" Percy remarked.

"We've blocked out the light so now, we just need to flood the roots, and remove its nutrients and oxygen," Daisy said, counting on her fingers as though trying to drum the understanding into herself. "How do we remove oxygen? Blast it into outer space?"

"If you could, that'd be great," Percy replied sarcastically.

"I left my spaceship in my other dungarees."

They turned their heads down the hallway, towards the kitchen and the staircase leading to the cellar. Suddenly, Daisy's nose wrinkled. She sniffed once and then again. "Bleurgh!"

Percy was about to ask her what was wrong but the odour hit him moments later. "Yuck! What is that stench?"

From a nearby room, the bells that announced the family's mealtimes began to jingle.

"Oh, no!" they cried. "It's lunch!"

Despite the smell, the thought of their father cooking away happily in the kitchen sent them a boost and they ran down the wide corridor and almost skidded into the kitchen. The room was filled with wisps of smoke and the pong of something terrible being done to mushrooms.

At the far side stood their father. He was leaning over the stove, stirring a frying pan with one hand and mashing a bowl of something disgusting with the other.

"Lunch is almost ready, children. Take a seat,"

he announced happily, not looking up from the task at hand. He added a pinch from one of his homemade spice jars into the pan. There was a sizzle and a cloud of thick, foul-smelling smoke bloomed from the pan.

"Father, we need your help; Mother needs your help," Percy began, and Father's head immediately swivelled round on his long neck. However, the smoke that was filling the room caught in the back of Percy's throat and made him cough.

Father stopped his stirring and mashing and sprinkling. "What? What's wrong with your mother?" he asked, suddenly serious.

"There's a plant taking over the house," Daisy tried but she, too, began to cough and splutter before she could finish her sentence. "Dad, can we get some more air in here?" she choked.

Just then, it was like a lightbulb flashed on in Percy's brain. Maybe, just maybe, Father's knack for completely ruining every meal he turned his hand to could actually be put to good use.

"No!" said Percy. He wafted away the smoke from in front of his face and tried not to breathe too deeply. "Father, we need you to turn the oven heat right up. Whatever you just added to that dish, add more of it! The hotter this house gets, the worse it'll be for the plant."

Father nodded. Percy was grateful that he accepted his son's request without any further questions and began to violently shake the contents of the glass jar into the pan, causing huge plumes of smoke and steam to erupt from the top of the stove. Father turned a few dials and the oven seemed to roar like a raging dragon. Hot air belched out of its mouth and Percy instantly felt the kitchen starting to heat up.

Suddenly, there was a *crash* from above them and the thick, spiralling vines of the psychivorum broke through the ceiling. It was fighting back.

Now out of spice mix, in a flash, Father snatched up an item just out of sight on the tiled counter. He raised a small glass bottle with a cork stopper, yanked the cork free with his mouth and spat it to the floor. "Take that! And that!" he cried as he poured a dark red liquid into the pan.

The kitchen was now almost completely hidden in smoke. Daisy's eyes were streaming and Percy could feel the sweat dripping down his face.

Percy watched as the vines of the psychivorum that hung through the crack in the ceiling writhed and fought against the heat. The largest began to wither, curl up and crumble.

"Not enjoying those chillies, eh?" Father laughed. "There are nineteen varieties, you know!"

Finally, juddering and fighting against its own downfall, the vine fell free of the ceiling and onto the dining room table, crushing the berries in the knitted fruit bowl. The ancient wood that had survived a lifetime under the sea, and many years of Father's cooking, gave way under the weight of the psychivorum's crumbling, dying vine.

Percy laughed silently and turned to his sister. If anyone would be relieved at the sight of the kitchen lying in ruin, it would be Daisy.

When he turned, however, she was gone. All that lay in her place were shredded floorboards and her toolbelt caught on a piece of torn wood.

# Chapter Eleven

"Daisy! Daisy!" Percy called.

There was no reply from his sister.

Percy's head started to swim with panic. He peered through the hole in the floorboards but he could see nothing but pitch-black darkness. Had the psychivorum taken her? Had their attacks on its sources of light and oxygen caused it to ramp up its search for nutrients? It already had Mother but maybe it now needed something more. Percy shuddered at the thought.

**117**

Percy picked up what remained of her toolbelt, tied it around his waist and turned. "Father, did you see where Daisy went?"

"Hmm?" his father said, distracted by the branch of the psychivorum that had shattered his kitchen.

Percy coughed on the air that was still thick and smoky. "I'm going to find Daisy. I need you to make the house as hot as possible. Use any and every ingredient you have!"

"Wonderful idea, son!" Father cried, dashing to the scullery and grabbing as many armfuls of jars and boxes and containers as he could carry.

"The plant will try to defend itself, Father, like it did here in the kitchen." Father acknowledged Percy's warning and then he made for the door, throwing handfuls of spice mix in all directions and turning knobs on the hallway heaters.

Percy passed by what remained of the psychivorum vine and headed for the cellar. Standing at the top of the downward staircase, looking into the darkness, Percy felt like he was about to step into a monstrous, hungry mouth.

"She would do it for me," he said to himself as he walked down into the darkness of the cellar, one slow, creaky step at a time. He reached for the toolbelt attached to his waist and found Daisy's torch.

Since he had taken a clipping of the plant the day before, the psychivorum had been nothing but trouble. It had broken and battered his home, and it had taken at least one member of his family. Would it now only be a matter of time before it came for him, too?

He gulped as he reached the bottom of the stairs. "Daisy?" he tried to whisper but, in the emptiness, his voice seemed to echo around the entire room.

Hearing a groaning coming from one of the storage rooms, Percy's skin seemed to tingle with a mix of relief and fear. As quietly as he could, he followed the sound on tiptoe. Shining his torch around the space, he could see that the door to the room was hanging open loosely and had a faint glow of light surrounding it.

With his heart in his mouth, he gently pushed open the creaking door. Light from the hole in the ceiling streamed in and down, illuminating a figure lying sprawled on the concrete floor.

"Daisy!" Percy rushed over to her. Her eyes were flickering and she was moaning softly. "Daisy!" He crouched down beside her, held the torch in his mouth and gently shook her shoulders. "Daisy! Are you OK?" he said, forcing the words around the handle of the torch.

She groaned once more and then, ever so slightly, opened one eye. "Will you get that torch out of my face!" She lifted her arms to slap the torch out of Percy's mouth.

Percy gave an enormous sigh of relief. "I thought the plant had got you!" he told her as he helped her up.

"No, it was the flippin' woodworm," she replied, brushing the dirt off her dungarees and inhaling deeply. "One minute, I was nearly being choked to death by that awful smoke in the kitchen. Then, the next thing I knew, the floorboards gave way and I ended up here." She shook her

120

head. "Tell you what though, Petal, this plant isn't giving up without a fight."

"I know," Percy said, "but we're almost there, now. We've got Grandmother blocking out the light, Father's making the house as hot as possible and so now, all that's left is..." He paused and pointed out of the doorway in the general direction of the boiler room, as though the plant might be able to hear their plan. "It's the only way we'll be able to save Mother."

"Well, what are we waiting for?" Daisy responded. She grabbed another torch off the toolbelt that was still wrapped around Percy's waist and headed back into the main room of the cellar.

Together, they stood outside the boiler room, torches ready and determination in their eyes. They pushed open the door and took in the sight that now greeted them.

The roots of the psychivorum had consumed the boiler room completely. Percy could make out the spot in the ceiling where the stem had grown throughout the rest of the house. Where the stem, the vines and the berries were filling various rooms of Poll Manor, making this habitat their own, the roots of the plant were left completely exposed.

"Pass me my wrench," Daisy said darkly, eyeing up the copper pipes and valves lining the cellar walls. She held out her hand expectantly.

"Um..." Percy looked down at the toolbelt around his waist. "A wrench..." he muttered.

"Oh, here!" Daisy snapped impatiently.

Selecting a large, steel spanner, she strode towards the ancient boiler and started to unscrew various parts of the plumbing, whacking at the plant's roots as she did so.

Suddenly, the door behind them crashed open, smashing in its frame. Huge vines punctured through the rotten wood and aimed for the closest child. Percy backed up and away until he stood flat against one of the walls. He could just make out five twisted tendrils closing in, ready to make a pincushion out of him.

Neither Daisy nor Percy dared to move. Breathing hard, Percy looked at his sister and at the root system throbbing and pulsating behind her. It had grown and it had developed. It had taken the best of everything from Poll Manor and it didn't belong here. Now, thanks to the family's efforts, it was like a wounded animal desperately trying to defend itself.

Never taking his eyes off the vines that were pointing menacingly at him like arrows suspended in mid-air, Percy fumbled at the toolbelt around his middle and grabbed at the largest, heaviest object he could find: a claw hammer.

Slowly, he removed it from the belt and then, gathering up all his strength, he lifted the hammer and with one great swing, hit one of the pipes that ran along the low ceiling of the boiler room.

The noise caused the psychivorum's vines to turn, react and thrash against the wall. The mortar, weakened through years of neglect and leaky pipes, began to crumble and collapse. A large section of ceiling near the boiler fell away and so did the floorboards and contents from the room above, trapping the tendrils underneath the pile of rubble. Water poured from the damaged pipes into the room in fierce streams and plaster rained down in heavy clumps.

Withering in the heat of Father's kitchen, weak from Grandmother's blackout painting and drowning in the slowly flooding cellar, the plant desperately clung to life. There was now only one thing making this house a home to the psychivorum and that was its food source – Mother.

Percy looked hard at his sister. "You stay with the roots. I need to go and see to Mother."

"Yeah. Finish this thing off, Petal. There's a lot more that I can do down here." Daisy grabbed the toolbelt off her brother and positioned it securely once more around her middle.

As Percy turned to find the stairs back up into the house, he saw his sister beginning to climb the walls of the cellar towards hard-to-reach pipes.

# Chapter Twelve

Percy dashed up through the manor, which was now almost unrecognisable. Holding his sleeve over his mouth and nose, he sprinted through the kitchen, where Father's stove-top disaster was gradually filling the ground floor with smoke. He pelted up the first flight of stairs and onto the landing, where the heat intensified and he began to sweat. He hurtled past his own bedroom door, through which he could see the blacked-out windows and the jungle of psychivorum leaves. Each one had now turned a sickly shade of yellow and many had fallen limply to the floor.

As he ran, Percy caught sight of his family. Father was opening doors, blocking up chimneys and adding fuel to the stove in the form of black garlic and peanut brittle. Grandmother had emptied all of her tins of black paint but was improvising by shifting her largest portraits around to cover cracks where sunlight might get through, while Bratwurst snapped and snarled at the waves of plant vines that were trying to stop her. As they worked feverishly to cut off the psychivorum's basic needs, each one battled against several long, slithering vines which seemed to have been drawn to the damage they were causing. Percy could only hope that this meant that Mother was no longer so well guarded.

Finally, panting, he skidded to a halt outside his mother's bedroom door. It was closed and no sound was coming from within.

How long had it been since he and Daisy had first gone looking for their mother? Percy felt his hands trembling as he reached for the door handle, imagining all kinds of terrible scenes that might be on the other side. What if he was too late?

It was surprising, considering the level of destruction that Poll Manor was now straining under, that Mother's bedroom door opened without a sound. Percy took a step into the room and was met by a sight so eerie that it made the hairs on the back of his neck stand on end.

The room was still and silent. The writhing tendrils were nowhere to be seen and the chaos that reigned throughout the rest of the house seemed to fall away behind Percy as he inched towards Mother.

She lay peacefully on top of her neatly folded bedsheets. To all the world, she might have appeared to be asleep, if it hadn't been for the single, enormous, purple-green tendril that lay snaked like a boa constrictor across the bedroom floor, oozing purple sap. Where the tip of the thick, glistening vine met the figure on the bed, it divided and wound its way around Mother's wrists and ankles, binding her there. Every few seconds, it seemed to heave and ripple, as though it were swallowing and passing something along its length.

As he tiptoed, his heart in his mouth, towards the foot of the bed, Percy kept his eyes on the psychivorum and wondered if it knew that he was here. This one giant limb seemed to have a different purpose from the ones rampaging through the manor, trying to finish off its attackers. It reminded Percy of a hose or a cable, plugged into his mother and pulling some kind of energy from her... but how much of an endless power source was she? Percy's insides felt heavy as he gazed at his mother's face and imagined her emptied of all her thoughts and feelings. He thought of the purple sap that was inside the stem of the enormous plant, carrying the plant's 'nutrients' to its leaves and roots.

Percy knew that once he began to attack the psychivorum and loosen its hold on Mother, he would not have much time before the plant realised what he was doing and returned to guard its food source. Percy kneeled by the side of the bed and whispered, "Mother?"

Nothing happened. Percy strained his ears to listen for movement below but, clearly, the plant was too distracted by Grandmother, Father and Daisy to notice him. Readying himself, he took a deep breath and began to prise the long, curling tendrils from around his mother's feet.

The second Percy touched the psychivorum, its grip around Mother tightened. Percy heard a mighty crash somewhere below him and knew that he had attracted the plant's attention. Sweating, he tugged desperately at Mother's bonds but they would not break, and no sooner had he finished untying one and moved onto another than the first immediately relaced itself around another part of her body. With each wriggling, purple cord that Percy untied, yet more noise tore through the house towards him. He knew that he only had seconds in which to act.

Under the threatening echoes of the psychivorum crashing its way through the walls of his home, breaking windows, dropping chandeliers and tearing carpets, however, Percy's ears picked up another sound. It was a motor, or an engine, or perhaps a small steam train – and it was getting louder. Whatever it might be was travelling at speed along the corridors in his direction.

Then, the ceiling of his parents' bedroom began to shake and dust rained down on top of Percy and Mother. Percy's progress was halted as he watched the floorboards around his feet explode upwards and vines, like the tentacles of an enormous creature, punched up through the floor and into the air, towering feet above his head and bearing down upon him. Seconds before they shot towards him, the motorised whirring from the corridor reached full volume... and the strangest sight yet appeared in the doorway.

Professor Devereux was dressed from head to toe in his Japanese karuta armour and carrying his long katana. Panels of black, rectangular plates covered most of his body, connected by chains and decorated with gold. He wore a metal helmet with a peak at the front, a long neck guard at the back and an ornate attachment stuck on top. He looked like an oversized beetle. As he rolled into the room in a flurry of metal arms and machinery, his expression was filled with determination and excitement.

"Take up arms!" he shouted, brandishing his sword. "Beat them back, young master!"

Percy gaped. It was enough of a surprise to see the professor outside of his living quarters or the library, let alone wearing anything other than his suit and bow tie. While the professor began to hack at the vines that had burst through the walls, Percy shook himself and frantically set about untying Mother from the bed once more. His heart was racing and his fingers were slippery with sweat but every time one of the psychivorum's vines came near him, another robotic arm from the professor's incredible wheelchair swooped in. The chair seemed to be doing the work of ten samurai warriors – limbs whirring in all directions, it gripped the plant's tendrils between pincers, pinned them to the floor under large, hammer-like attachments and held them back with jets of steam that sizzled when they hit.

"Have at you, beast!" yelled the professor, who seemed to be enjoying himself immensely.

Percy felt as though he were playing a bizarre game of whack-a-mole. Time and time again, he removed one of the vines around Mother and turned to the next, only to find that his previous work had already been undone. He tried pinning

the plant down with his knees, feet and even the top of his head but it was no good – he needed Mother's help.

"Mother!" Percy cried, ducking under the psychivorum's swinging arms. He shook her but she was as limp as a rag doll.

Glaring at her untroubled expression, Percy felt his eyes filling with frustrated tears. He thought about his sherbet-covered bedsheets and about how Mother had always been there for him, to love him in her own way. As his insides filled with warmth, Percy racked his brain and leant in close to her.

"Mother," he said gently, his voice hidden under the chaos that the professor's chair was causing. "Mother, you need to wake up. The pillows need turning."

A tendril of the psychivorum lashed towards Percy and he dived out of its way. When he scrambled to his feet, he could feel a trickle of warm blood on his cheek. He looked hopefully at Mother but her eyes were still closed.

Across the room, the professor was tiring. His armour was missing in some places; several of the chair's arms lay snapped and broken on the floor and steam was whistling out from puncture holes in its sides.

His face stinging, Percy grasped his mother's hand. "Mother!" he pleaded. "Wake up! The carpet needs to be polished!"

Ears ringing, Percy gasped as he felt his mother's hand squeezing his own. At the same moment, another tendril crashed down beside him, coating Percy in dust and splinters. Feeling giddy in the knowledge that he was onto something, he leapt aside as the plant swiped furiously left and right and as the professor's chair was lifted from the ground by its wheels.

"The books on the bookshelves need colouring in!" panted Percy, dancing around the plant's outstretched limbs and the damage to the bedroom floor. Across the room, the professor was dangling upside down, sword in hand, shouting, "Unhand me, you scoundrel!"

The bedroom floor groaned under the weight of

the damage but, finally, Mother was stirring. Percy raised his voice. "The bath mats haven't been ironed!" he yelled, looking left and right for a way out as he was backed against the wall by three flailing vines. "The mice haven't had their bedtime story and... and... *and the heating's gone up to twenty-nine degrees!*" he screamed, catching sight of the bedroom thermometer. Percy pressed himself into the corner of the room, waiting for the psychivorum to strike.

# Chapter Thirteen

On the bed, Mother's eyes snapped open. The psychivorum seemed to freeze in shock and, at that moment, Percy ducked under one of its branches and ran back to his mother. As he pulled the plant from each of her wrists and ankles, he watched a little more life return to her face and she began to struggle against the psychivorum.

Across the room, Professor Devereux was gaining the upper hand. With every piece of Mother that was released, it seemed that the psychivorum lost more energy. Inch by inch, the professor's chair was lowered back to the wooden floor and the attacking tendrils wilted and drooped until, finally, they gave a great shudder and fell limply to the ground. Percy's mother wrenched herself out of the bed and folded her arms around him.

"Petal," she said softly. She looked weak, like a flower that had been trampled underfoot. Then, she frowned. "Petal, why on earth do you have whiskers on your face?"

The noise around them quietened gradually, leaving only the creaks of the straining walls and ceilings and the gentle whirring and rattling of the professor's badly beaten wheelchair. Percy watched as the thick, cable-like branch of the psychivorum shrivelled back from Mother's bed, turning wrinkled and dry before his eyes.

"Victory!" exclaimed Professor Devereux, who looked delighted beneath his coating of dust and cloud of steam. "Those devils were no match for us, eh, Master Percival? Why, back in Crimea, I –"

"Oh, give it a rest, you old windbag," snapped

a voice.

Grandmother shuffled into the room, Bratwurst at her heels. She, too, looked rather pleased with herself, despite being covered in black, oily smudges. She looked around the bedroom and raised her finely pencilled eyebrows. "I do hope somebody is going to clean this up."

"Lady Poll," the professor bowed his head and twirled his hand dramatically.

"Don't you 'Lady Poll' me!" Grandmother said in a withering tone. "You wouldn't know good manners if they came and bit you on the bottom!"

Percy chuckled. His mother held him at arm's length and looked him up and down. "What on earth have you been up to, Petal?" she asked.

Percy explained how the whole family had worked together to distract the plant long enough to rescue Mother and that, now Poll Manor had been made such a terrible environment for the plant to live in, it would have no choice but to leave. When he reached the part about

Father and Daisy, he stopped. A new wave of uncertainty washed over him and he said, "We have to find them."

Leaving Grandmother and the professor to their bickering, Percy took his mother's hand and guided her from the room. Together, they walked through the ruined corridors of Poll Manor, gazing at the damage and stopping every so often to allow Mother to straighten a painting.

Grandmother had been busy – every window that they passed was coated in thick, oily paint or a framed portrait and there was little sunlight left at all. When they passed Percy's bedroom window, they saw that the jungle of enormous leaves had fallen to the floor, colourless and brittle. The house was also stiflingly hot and, when they reached the kitchen, they could see why.

The kitchen had been destroyed. Father's stovetop disaster had left one side of the room completely coated in soot, melted utensils and burnt ingredients. The smell was truly terrible and Percy could see parts of the psychivorum's stem through the torn wallpaper, coated in dust and ash. Without enough oxygen coming in through its stem and roots, the plant would have relied upon its leaves to produce it – and they had taken care of those already.

There was no sign of Father, and Percy began to feel nervous. "Daisy?" he called. "Father?"

"In here," said a familiar voice.

Percy felt a ripple of relief run from the top of his head to his toes. He let go of Mother's hand and raced into the orangery, following Daisy's voice. He found her and Father standing facing opposite sides of the stiflingly hot room. In her hands, Daisy was holding a hammer and a piece of copper piping, and Father was carrying a large saucepan. They were both very still and had the look of two people waiting to corner a house spider.

"Are you OK?" he asked the pair.

"We're fine," Daisy whispered, without taking her eyes from the mess of leaves and trunks which covered the orangery walls. She looked drenched from head to foot and Percy guessed that her work in the cellar had been a success.

"Why are we whispering?"

Daisy and Father stood back to back, turning in slow circles. "It's in here somewhere," Daisy breathed.

Percy took a closer look around the room, searching for a glimpse of purple.

"I saw it," Daisy continued, "in the cellar. It sort of... detached itself... and went running up into the kitchen. Dad managed to trap it in here but now, we've lost it."

For a moment, the three of them stood in the centre of the room in deadly silence, hardly daring to breathe.

Then, suddenly, Mother breezed into the room from the kitchen. "Basil!" she called happily. "Flower. I've missed you!" Gliding towards them, she planted a kiss on each of their cheeks and then waltzed towards the orangery doors. "It's awfully hot in here, my dears," she said and, oblivious to her family's outbursts of shock, threw the double doors open.

"Mother! No!" shouted Percy, but he was too late. As a wave of cool, clean air rushed into the house, the branches of the date palm in the corner rustled and a blur of purple leaves darted towards the doorway.

"After it!" yelled Daisy.

They tore out of the orangery after the little plant, blinking away the bright sunlight. The psychivorum looked only a little bigger now than it had when Percy had found it; several small, spindly roots held it above the ground and a measly stem supported only a handful of rather pathetic-looking, purple leaves. It was as though the plant had discarded its dying leaves and roots, leaving the bare essentials. It was light, however, and very fast.

Percy and Daisy chased the psychivorum down across the open lawn, sprinting over the grass just as they had the morning before. Percy's muscles were burning as he ran.

"We can't risk this thing coming back," Daisy shouted from behind him.

Percy's mind was working almost as hard as his legs. Daisy was right – as soon as they had put the house back together and the environment would support it once more, the psychivorum would return. They chased it over the flowerbeds, around the greenhouses and down towards the winding path that led to the lake. How on earth were they going to catch it?

An answer arrived in a flurry of white and blue. Percy was just starting to wonder how much longer his legs would be able to continue when what appeared to be a very small sailor burst out of a hedgerow to Percy's left.

"Bratwurst!" panted Percy.

The little dog's legs were almost impossible to see as he flew along the path. The trio were closing in on the psychivorum, which now had no choice but to turn towards the edge of the lake. With water to one side, Bratwurst to the other and Daisy and Percy behind it, the plant tore along the bank as fast as its roots could carry it.

Up ahead, the sweeping gardens gave way to thick, overgrown woodland. Percy knew that once the plant reached the trees, they would lose sight of it. He forced his legs to move faster than they had ever moved before but, as the treeline grew closer, he felt panic rising in his chest.

The psychivorum, as if it knew safety was close, thrust itself along the lakeside away from Percy. As it made the last few bounds towards the cool shade of the woodland, the waters of the lake stirred.

CRASH. The surface of the lake broke with a sound like a gunshot and at least a dozen huge tentacles burst free. A blue-grey limb, like an enormous whip, lashed across the ground and wrapped itself around the psychivorum. Then, from beneath the once-still water, a huge, domed head emerged.

"KRAKEN!" Percy screamed.

The colossal sea creature lifted the psychivorum with its tentacle, observed it up close with one of its bulbous eyes and, in one fluid, whirlwind movement, dragged it down into the watery depths of the lake.

For what felt like the longest time, Percy, Daisy and Bratwurst stood in shock and stared at the glassy surface of the lake.

Finally, Percy muttered a few words under his breath. "I *knew* it."

# Chapter Fourteen

Back inside what remained of Poll Manor, Percy found his family up to their usual business. Mother was busy sorting different types of rubble depending on their size, shape and weight. She also had one of the psychivorum's vines tossed loosely about her neck like a fine scarf. Apparently, Percy's words had instilled in her a very long to-do list and she needed to get busy. Percy left her in the kitchen, trying to find the flattest stones possible to use as plates for supper that night.

"At least now, you can tell Grandmother that the Queen's plates have been destroyed without getting me in trouble," Percy had said.

Percy came across Grandmother wandering the corridors, observing the black paint splattered across the windows. "Hmm... not bad," she remarked, and straightened a portrait of Bratwurst dressed as a sunflower. The little dachshund stood by her side, slipping and sliding on the slicks of black paint like a living bowling ball.

Professor Devereux emerged from the library as the longcase clock chimed. Looking completely unscathed, he was back in his pristine three-piece suit and had even combed his beard. His chair no longer showed any kind of damage; it was as though the day's events had not happened. "Master Percival, it is time for your lessons," he wheezed.

"Lessons?" Percy exclaimed. "Professor, the whole house has been destroyed."

"That is no excuse," Professor Devereux replied. "Collect your trombone and I shall see you shortly."

Percy decided that he would find his trombone and make sure it had not survived the collapse of Poll Manor. He made his way down the cellar steps to find Daisy. Halfway down, tangled in the ruins and no longer a threat, lay a discarded vine of the psychivorum. Slipping slightly on the fallen rubble, Percy's foot went straight through the weed and came up sticky.

The cellar was almost unrecognisable and, if anything, smelt even worse than the kitchen. It looked as though Daisy had managed to unscrew every nut and valve in the place. Waist-deep, murky water filled the space, submerging the roots of the psychivorum. Where Percy could see parts of the plant, he noticed that they had rotted already.

Father was in one corner, wearing waders and taking slices from what remained of the psychivorum. Percy hoped that it would not make it into tonight's stew. He splashed into the lukewarm water, wrinkling his nose, and made his way to the boiler room.

The boiler itself had been destroyed. Where the roots of the plant had not punctured it, it looked as though Daisy's tools had. Water was still slowly gushing from various places and the roots had turned yellow-brown and mushy.

"Hey, Flower," Percy said, wading into the room.

She turned and scowled. "Hey, Petal," she replied, grinding his nickname between her teeth. She was standing with her hands on her hips, looking at the crushed and shattered remains of the boiler. Without it, the house had no running water and no heating.

"Is there anything you can do for it?" Percy asked.

She smiled. "Oh, you know me, Petal. I can fix anything if I put my mind to it."

*

A little while later, Percy took himself out into the grounds of the manor and strolled among the agapanthuses and the hydrangeas, enjoying the fresh air. There was still a lot of work to do at the house but it wasn't going anywhere.

He did a lap of the lawns and then, on a bench down by the lake, pulled out his grandfather's journal and wondered for a while about how he might recreate those perfect lawn borders.

Sometime later, Percy looked out over the rippling surface of the lake and thought back over the events of the past two days. He thought about his mother, who had been saved from a terrible fate by her remarkable, if odd, family. He thought about the psychivorum, which had been so desperate to live in Poll Manor.

Well, thought Percy, he could hardly blame it. He stared fondly up at the house, with its blacked-out windows and smoking chimneys. He could see Father through the kitchen window, shaking soot out of his pots and pans. Mother was out on the patio, beating one of the hallway carpets with a ladle. Percy imagined that he could see Daisy draining buckets of water out of the cellar, Grandmother forcing

Bratwurst into his next outfit and the professor planning his lessons, watched over by his suit of armour. He thought about each and every member of his peculiar family, and a warmth spread through him from his fingertips to his toes as he walked peacefully back up the path towards home.

**How much can you remember about the story? Take this quiz to find out!**

1 What breed of dog is Bratwurst?

2 What is the name of the Poll family's live-in tutor?

3 What special nutrient does the psychivorum need?

4 What is Percy's nickname?

Answers: 1. dachshund/sausage dog 2. Professor Devereux 3. human thoughts 4. Petal

## Challenge

There are many different species of plant mentioned in this story.

Can you find 6 species of plant hidden in this wordsearch?

| I | Q | A | P | R | S | N | Y |
|---|---|---|---|---|---|---|---|
| B | V | A | F | O | M | E | N |
| W | L | S | S | S | F | N | O |
| M | V | N | O | E | I | X | E |
| E | N | I | M | S | A | J | P |
| P | C | O | N | I | F | E | R |
| N | A | I | R | E | L | A | V |
| O | K | X | O | G | Z | R | F |

# Discussion Time

**?** Would you like to live at Poll Manor?
Why or why not?

**?** 'For as long as Percy could remember, Daisy had
spent her life keeping things together.' Why do you
think Daisy has felt the need to do this?

**?** How do the Poll family work together to defeat
the psychivorum?

**?** How do you think Percy feels about his family? Find
evidence in the text to support your opinion.

## Discover more from Twinkl Originals...

Continue the learning! Explore the library of Percy Poll's
Peculiar Plants activities, games and classroom resources at
twinkl.com/originals

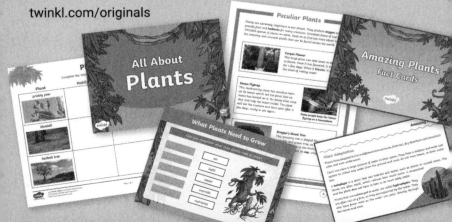

# Welcome to the world of Twinkl Originals!

## Board books
**Ages 0-3**

## Picture books
**Ages 3-7**

## Longer stories
**Ages 7-11**

### Books delivered to your door

Enjoy original works of fiction in beautiful printed form, delivered to you each half term and yours to keep!

1. **Join the club** at **twinkl.com/book-club**

2. Sign up to our **Ultimate membership**.

3. **Make your selection** – we'll take care of the rest!

### The Twinkl Originals app

Now, you can read Twinkl Originals stories on the move! Enjoy a broad library of Twinkl Originals eBooks, fully accessible offline.

Search '**Twinkl Originals**' in the App Store or on Google Play.

# Look out for the next Book Club delivery

**It's the Saturday that Demi has been waiting for: one of the world's biggest stars is coming to Sheffield.**

But when the concert is threatened by a terrible theft, and the main suspect has been locked in Sheffield's famous green police box the entire time, it's up to Demi and her dads to solve the clues and crack this curious case wide open...

Coming May 2022

**Can't wait?**
Get the digital version at
**twinkl.com/originals**